One Day
in Church Kirk

D P Robinson

St James Church, Church Kirk

Talbot

Rishton

Text & Cover © Derek P Robinson 2023
All rights reserved.

Contents:

Also, by the same author:

Don't Lose Your Cap: *Four short stories full of action and adventure.*

Ricky Rishton, in paperback and *eBook: A short story telling of Ricky Rishton's ride in the World championship road race and other poems about cycling, conceived while out on the road putting in the miles.*

The Black Curtain: eBook: *Four poems about a rock n' roll go-go bar.*

Dedicated to Shirley, Frank Whittaker, Roy Sleddon, Douglas Hartley and Roy Tattersall.

Acknowledgments.

I am grateful to the many people who walked with me on this day. A special thanks to Michael Hodkinson for his readings and suggestions.

Church Kirk?

Situated in Lancashire, north-west England, the name of this parish hamlet has been a puzzle to many people!

On his way to meet the Mercians at Oswestry, the King of Northumbria, St. Oswald, stopped by a spring-well because his army would need a plentiful supply of fresh water. To fulfil his need for a place of worship, Oswald built here a field kirk, or small wooden place of worship, from where he or one of his monks could give service, calling this place 'Kirk.'

Oswald was slain on August 5, AD 642, when, during the Battle of Maserfield on the Welsh Marches, the pagan Mercians conquered Oswald's kingdom. Eventually, the Mercians' themselves became Christians and called Kirk 'Church.'

Therefore, Kirk is Northumbrian and Church is Mercian; hence, Church Kirk, which is *the only place or town to be named after a place of worship.*

Today, in place of that wooden place of worship, at the heart of Church Kirk, surrounded by grey headstones, some of great age, and fronted by mature sycamore trees, the resting place for corbies and larks, stands the stone-built St. James' Church.

Built around AD 1250, the oldest part of St. James' church, the bell tower was used as a watchtower by the Rishton's in their sour battles with the Talbots during the 'Wars of Roses.'

Each side held a different political stand; the Rishton's supported the 'House of Lancaster' whereas the Talbots took sides with the 'House of York.' *

But as Billy Rishton is about to discover, this place was founded long before St. Oswald passed this way...

Chapter 1

October 1957

in Billy Rishton's Study.

Situated between the main railway line and the steam engine workshop, the neglected rusty hinges groan and the cold, brisk wind rattles the corrugated tin roof when rail stock apprentice Billy Rishton pushes the rotting door of the red brick toilet inward. Behind the door, hanging from a nail via a loop of sugar string, a yellow travel magazine scrapes an arc across the holly green paint.

Swearing, as he did on each visit, to one day "fix those bloody hinges and give them a good oiling," Billy trips the Bakelite switch. The bare bulb illuminates the wood-built, long drop toilet. Careful not to spill any precious hot tea, he lovingly places his Flying Scotsman mug on the small shelf, strategically placed to be within easy reach when seated.

Using the instep of his left boot under the jagged door, with both hands under the centre stile, he gently lifts and drops the door closed on its latch.

He turns around and after wiping the toilet seat with a half page of the Accrington Observer, he wrestles off his blue boiler suit. Placing his goose pimpled cheeks on the mahogany seat, he smiles when he feels it's still warm from the previous student.

He takes a sip of tea, then reaches out and unhooks the yellow dog-eared magazine. This has become his friend during the monotonous grey days at the bleak railway sidings. A friend with whom he escapes the drudgery of scraping filthy black soot out of the steam engine boilers and roams into other worlds until now unknown to an eighteen-year-old from Lettuce Row, Church Kirk.

Reading a few pages each day, it has taken Billy two months to arrive at the final story in the well-thumbed magazine. The short story, re-printed from the works of the missionary monk Paulinus, has taken him back fifteen hundred years into the dark ages of English history and will complete what has been a fascinating horizon-broadening journey.

Elbows on knees, Billy reads on.

"During the Anglo-Saxon conquest of England in AD449, the British Chieftain, Vortigern, invited two Saxons, Hengist and Horsa, to help him repel invasions of the Picts and Scots. The successful Saxons, instead of returning to their own country, settled in England and in time, showing a brand of treachery unknown to the peace-loving Britons, turned on their hosts and, with the Picts and Scots, drove them into the west of England."

"While fleeing from these treacherous Saxons, a tribe of Christian Britons led by their chieftain, Dagda, happened upon a fertile area of land in the north west of England that plays host to a fresh spring well above a picturesque, densely wooded valley. Weary from their journey, with his wife, Creirwy, son Ogma and daughter Mary, Dagda decided to set up camp and see if they could build a home in this quiet, picturesque place."

"Soon after settling, realising their livestock and crops prospered, as did the plants surrounding the spring well, and their own health thrived. In the early days of Christianity, the superstitious Britons were quick to link nature and religion. They imagined the water to have magical powers and streams of pilgrims arrived, seeking cures from the spring water."

"Mary was the one to collect and serve the water to the pilgrims, insisting on receiving it in the silver chalice made by her father."

"They believed that her long blond hair, which blended with the yellow of her embroidered saffron-dyed tunic, her eyes with the clover, her gentleness, purity and beauty, all added to the water's power. Over the years, the well and Mary's reputation grew."

"This veneration worried her father and though he kept his concern to himself, he feared one-day she may be accused of witchery and some awful fate would befall her."

"Over the years, Dagda had built a family house and farm buildings; he had ploughed land, a meadow and a small orchard attached.

Other farmers copied his methods and good relationships were established and maintained. All was well between neighbouring farmers who would get together where needed: constructing and/or repairing buildings, cutting down trees, gathering fruit, making ale, or helping to carry heavy loads. Until one Sunday..."

"Towards the middle of the day when celebrations for the harvest festival were reaching a peak, marauding through the north west in search of Christian Britons, a band of Saxon heathens attacked. Confusion reigned, and with the sight of gold and silver crucifixes adding venom to their blood lust, the heathens ran amok. All the villagers and any monks present were put to the sword despite their vain attempts to fight back. The well-armed Saxons were far too savage for the humble farmers.

"While the village was being ransacked, Dagda searched for his daughter and rushed her into a small niche he had secretly excavated within the spring well.

"Covering this hiding place with a reed frame and fresh cut branches, believing Mary to be safe, he hurried back to his house in search of his wife, but all he found was the horrible sight of her hanging from a pear tree, her body bloody, naked and helpless. Instantly his faith diminished and then three bearded axe-wielding warriors hacked him down.

"Unknown to Dagda, the Saxon chieftain Hengist had seen him shelter Mary. Dying on the ground, the distraught father reached out in anguish; his final sight was of his beloved Mary being dragged from the well by her famous blond hair. Tied to a stake in the centre of the village, Mary closed her eyes and prayed to her God. The rough collection of wood at her feet was set alight and her famous embroidered tunic was consumed in the flames.

"The Saxons final act was to set fire to houses, crops and meadows and their day's dirty work done, the weary heathens wiped their swords clean on the grass and ate supper, before leaving the plundered village.

"Two miles away, fishing on a lake near the hamlet of Rishton, Dagda's son, Ogma, and some other village fishermen saw the smoke billowing high above the village. Rushing back as fast their legs could carry them, with young Ogma leading the way, they arrived exhausted to find little was left of their once proud village.

"The setting sun dying the village a fiery red, Ogma looked through the devastated scene, searching for his family. All he found in the charred remains was his sister's silver crucifix. Carefully collecting Mary's ashes, Ogma placed them in the silver chalice she had used to feed water to her adoring pilgrims.

"After helping the other mourners to bury their loved ones, Ogma sealed the chalice with clay and horsehair then placed it inside the ill-fated niche within the spring well. Together with the few remaining villagers, he placed a stone slab over it, thus sealing Mary's burial chamber. With no monks surviving, it was Ogma who led the prayers and then, his duties and respects completed and vehemently vowing revenge on the Saxons, he turned his back on his home, declaring that no-one could now harm his beautiful sister and that no evil mouth could ever drink again the waters of this peaceful valley

"Mary's story, initially told by Ogma and his followers as they roamed around the west in search of Saxons, became coloured in the telling and over the years, legend and myth grew about her terrible fate.

"I heard Mary's story when as chaplain to Ethelburga, sister to the King of Kent, I came north to preach the Christian faith to her new husband, Edwin, the pagan King of Northumbria who, following his conversion, decreed that all Northumbria should become Christian. Cadwallon of Wales and King Penda of Mercia killed Edwin in the battle at Hatfield Chase, giving reason for my return to Kent together with Ethelburga. On my journey, I made a pilgrimage to search for Mary's grave. After several weeks travel, I found the place and the stone slab. I stood there and with a tearful heart, blessed the overgrown grey/green stone grave. Then in order to make it easier to find, should other pilgrims wish to pay their respects, I had the bare stone inscribed with …"

So absorbed in the story, Billy has forgotten all about his tea. Pausing from the tale, he lifts the mug from the shelf and takes a sip.

But it is cold and he instantly spits out the bitter liquid. Reaching to replace the mug on the shelf, the 10.35 express from Blackpool to Colne comes thundering past, shaking the foundations of the red outhouse. The vibration of the rumbling carriages makes it impossible for him to replace the mug on the shelf. To avoid any spillage, he raises his feet off the ground and holds his arms out to balance on the edge of the seat, his rear end soaking up the tremors. A Stanier 4-6-0 Class 5 locomotive and coal trucks roll by on the opposite line, rattling the corrugated roof and the soft human waste sloshes in the thunder box below. When the trains pass, he settles back down and, still holding on to his mug, returns to the story. Searching for his place on the page, he re-reads: "I had the bare stone inscribed with …"

Then suddenly the study door is pushed open, knocking the Scotsman out of his hand and splashing the cold tea on the open page; defacing the print. The Scotsman crashes into fragments on the flagstone floor, splattering his boots and boiler suit with the dregs of tea.

"Billy, Billy! Are you still in there?" shouts someone from outside, "foreman's looking for you."

Billy recognises the voice of his pal, Little Joe, and shouts back, "Hey! Hey! you pillock, you've smashed my bloody Scotsman."

Shaking the magazine free from excess tea, he dabs the wet pages with more of the Observer only to find the vital text is stained a milky brown. It's impossible to read the letters. Staring hard to interpret the last three words, he hears the foreman's voice outside asking Little Joe, "is that scrounger, Billy, still in there?"

The atmosphere in the study is filling with a pungent cloud rising from the agitated waste, and thinking he can just make out the first word, Billy hurriedly pulls up his pants and with the arms of his overalls tied at the waist, he carefully hoists the green door closed, hangs the latch and leaves the story of … Mary –? –? hanging in the dark.

Chapter 2

July 1967, Part 1

King Georges Hall

In the foyer of King George's Hall on this summer's evening, his hands crossed over the head of his cane, a very angry Gilbert Rishton says, "over my dead body."

"If needs be," says a calm but equally angry Robert Talbot, as he passes old Gilbert on his way to his theatre box.

Robert enjoys seeing the empty seats in the auditorium stalls and a self-satisfied grin spread across his fat red face. The immaculately dressed local businessman steps into his private box above the orchestra. Slowly, he feeds his large frame into his seat, checks the time on his gold watch and tucks it in the left pocket of the strained expanse of his scarlet waste coat.

Those in the stalls scornfully look up at the man who wants to rob them of their church.

King George V laid the foundation stone during his visit to Blackburn on July the 10th 1913. The Hall is built in the classical style from stone quarried at Butlers Delph in Pleasington. The frontage and the first-floor Corinthian columns over a three-arched entrance lead into the spacious entrance, from where music lovers are guided into the auditorium. While waiting in the wings for his introduction by the conductor, Sir Charles Groves of the 'Royal' Liverpool Philharmonic Orchestra, Mrs. Amelia Rishton adjusts the bowtie of her twenty-year-old son, Richard 'Ricky' Rishton.

On the front row, the Reverend Peter Samman sits proudly beside his stern-faced archdeacon. For weeks before this night, the Reverend has prayed that a good turnout will negate the Archdeacon's decision to close his ancient St. James' Church, Church Kirk.

A falling congregation and the need for repairs, plus the rising costs of upkeep, have led the church leaders to consider selling St. James'. But though the journey is slow and painful, such is their love for the church that the Reverend and Ricky's grandfather, old Gilbert, dragging his gammy leg, have spent many hours delivering flyers advertising the concert around the flagged streets of Church, Accrington and Oswaldtwistle.

As the churchwarden, Gilbert knows that Robert has made an offer. Moreover, if the rumour circulating is correct, he wants to expand his business and convert St. James' into a furniture warehouse. If losing the church isn't enough, the sale to a 'Talbot' doubly angers Gilbert, hence the heated altercation in the foyer.

Looking around the auditorium, expecting a full house, Gilbert rubs his hands and tries to calculate the takings at the door in his head. The church bell tower still stands derelict and the old bells are silent. Fully aware that most folk in Church Kirk remember their melodious sound. Gilbert wonders if there will be enough to pay the builders for the repairs necessary.

Now that the night for the concert has arrived, he is looking to forget his troubles and is eager to hear the progress his nephew, Ricky, has made during his time at the Royal Manchester College of Music. He's especially proud of him for agreeing to play and help raise funds for the church he has such fond memories of. Gilbert has convinced the Reverend that the silent congregation, who, although they don't attend the church as regularly as they would like, still hold beliefs and see the church with its venerable presence as the focal point of the village, The old church is close to their hearts, yet this night is not looking good for Gilbert; his hoped-for full house is scant and people are only trickling in in twos and threes.

The Reverend has also noticed the sparse auditorium and looks at Gilbert expectantly. Gilbert smiles back, trying to reassure the Reverend that more will come, as promised.

Robert grins widely. Comfortable in his seat, he is happy to see the empty seats. He hates being here and having to listen to this 'tripe' as he often says to his wife, Claudette, a petite black-haired beauty whom their only daughter Shirley takes after. Robert hates classical music and thinks the musicians are all wastrels and the audience is all phonies. In his gruff voice, he often tells Claudette, "The pursuit of money, that's what they should be doing, not this rubbish. Look at them pretending to understand this stuff, yaaah!" As always throughout their marriage, Claudette says nothing, suffering yet another of his angry outbursts.

Ricky, of average height, has brown shoulder length hair and hazel eyes. A gifted pianist, he is to play Rachmaninov's 'Rhapsody on a Theme from Paganini,' and in the second half, return to play the rare piano solo of 'Tchaikovsky's 1812 Overture'.

Last night, Amelia slept in her curlers, and it has taken her, with help from her daughters Jean and Edith, all day to dress for this evening. Standing in front of her son in her best frock, she makes the final touches to his tie. Then, brushing the invisible flecks off his hired tuxedo with a gentle sweep from the backs of her extended fingers and pinching his cheek, she whispers in an attempt to lift his spirits. She knows how much he is missing Shirley, his beloved girlfriend, but limits her exhortation to a simple "come on! Play it for your grandfather."

This is to be Ricky's debut at King George's Hall and although not one of the world's great concert arenas, he has always dreamt of playing at his local concert hall.

He feels self-conscious in the heavy tuxedo and his shirt collar is uncomfortable. It is too tight and threatens to cut off his air supply. He twitches, and although he has lost some of his broad north-east Lancashire accent whilst studying at the College of Music, he remembers he is still a local lad when he thinks, "I wish I were in my scruff!"

But this is to be Amelia's big night just as much as his, so there's no way he's going to disappoint her. As a result, he simply nods and mumbles, "All right, Mum." Ready to walk on to the stage and play, memories of his first music lesson on the organ in St. James' church while sitting on his grandfather's lap come floating back.

Chapter 3 1952

Gilbert Rishton.

Gilbert Rishton is a descendant of the Rishton family of Ponthalgh and Dunkenhalgh. An amiable man, he's wiry of stature with strong hands and body. Sharp blue eyes give away unexpected intelligence from someone who has spent many years labouring down the coal mines. The seams mapped across his face, he's a man engrossed in his music as he and Ricky play the hymn, 'How sweet the name of Jesus sounds," on the old church organ.

The first organ was bought at the suggestion of Robert Peel, affectionately called 'Fat Robert', who organised a meeting with other members of the parish to decide whether to have a peal of bells or a church organ. Robert proposed that if an organ is bought rather than a peal of bells, "People would have to come to church to hear it, whereas if they bought bells, any lazy fellow could lie in the fields and hear them." Robert's reasoning won the day and in 1815, an organ was built for £26. 6s 6d; being rebuilt and enlarged in 1849.

Playing with his grandfather is the inspiration for the adventurous young Ricky to study music. With today's lessons over, silver haired Gilbert, his leg serving him badly, steps down from the organ and smiles when he sees his son, Ricky's father, Edgar Rishton, enter the church, shaking rain from his overcoat. Black haired and stout, Edgar is a fireman, the one who explodes charges down the coalmine at the Thorney Bank Colliery drift mine, Hapton, near Burnley.

Gilbert's gold pocket watch chimes twelve bells to announce noon; the pub doors are open! On a wet but warm summer day, he shakes his head in despair at the pool of rainwater dripping through the holes in the church roof he has worshiped under since a boy. As a parish leader, he and the Reverend have pleaded with the Archdeacon to give them time to raise the necessary money. Every day before organ practice, he prays for a miracle.

"This's thirsty work," he says.

Wiping sweat from his brow with the back of his rough hand, Edgar greets his father with a handshake. "Come on, dad, let's have a drink at Thorn Inn," he says.

With his arms stretched to hold on to both his dad's and granddad's hands, Ricky walks down the long churchyard pathway.

Entering the inn, all three are greeted with the familiar smell of St. Bruno from the pipe of Bill Mather, the chubby, balding landlord.

"Owdo, Gil, Edgar, says Bill, not seeing little Ricky below the other side of the bar. Through nicotine-stained teeth, clenched tight gripping the stem of his mahogany barrelled pipe like a well-practised ventriloquist, the cheerful Bill asks, "What'll it be, usual?" his animated martial eyebrows giving away his previous occupation.

"All right, Bill," Edgar and Gilbert greet the Thwaites's tenant.

"Aye, usual and a lemonade for little un here," says Gilbert, patting Ricky gently on the head.

Knowing it will take a while for the creamy, mild beer to pour, the three generations of Rishtons settle down on wooden benches in the taproom of the eighteenth-century hostelry. Being in the centre of the terraced houses that make up this urban district, the inn is the hub of the community and acts as a meeting place for all ages. And, because Bill knows all their parents, the kids are allowed in and can buy drinks like sarsaparilla, dandelion, and burdock pop. They can also play on the newly arrived pinball machine if they have any money.

Bill brings the drinks in on a tin tray. Gilbert and Edgar swallow the whole pint in one gulp. Between them, Ricky stares in astonishment. Their thirst was partially quenched; they ordered a second pint. After a few minutes of general conversation, Edgar's eldest son, Ralph, comes in, looking for his dad.

"Ah, you are in. Mum says you'd be in here," says Ralph, who, being dark, takes more after his dad than his fair-haired mother.

Settling down by his grandfather's side with a glass of sarsaparilla, Ralph, a reluctant scholar, asks, "Do you know anything about Church Kirk?" He explains that his history teacher has given him an essay to complete on a local topic.

Gilbert, a self-educated man and local historian, says, "Why don't you tell the tale of the notorious Roger de Rishton? He is responsible for the missing relics from the church altar, you know?" "Relics! What are they?" asks Ralph.

"They're like antiques, old things," says Edgar, wanting to give his sons the impression he is as knowledgeable as their grandfather.

"Oh! Go on then," says Ralph, his interest pricked. "Roger, who?"

Gilbert removes his flat cap and places it carefully on the table next to his new pint of mild, his church troubles forgotten for the time being. "Roger de Rishton," he begins, "is the black sheep in our family and the biggest blackguard in Church Kirk's history."

"Hang on, granddad, what's "de" mean with "de Rishton?" Ralph asks, thinking he had better get the facts right in case his teacher asks him any questions.

"Oh, it means *of,* so it's Roger *of* Rishton, because that's where he originated from, all right?" replies Edgar.

"Oh, right," says Ralph, making a mental note.

Gilbert continues. "He gained his sordid reputation through acts of violence against the church when he was a young man of 22 years, in 1537, I think. Anyway, it was during the reign of Henry the Eighth. Roger, we'll drop the 'de Rishton' for now; he inherited the manor of Church when his dad, Ralph, died," Gilbert glanced at his grandson in recognition of his namesake. "And he went to live in the manor house where Mr. Henderson now lives at the top of Dunkenhalgh. Although in them days it was called Ponthalgh and some parts, such as the doorway and mullion windows, are still there, you must have seen them when you've been down there ratting."

Edgar and his two sons sit back and relax, resigning themselves to the fact that they have no option but to listen to yet another piece of folklore. Not that they mind. There are far worse things to be doing on a lazy Saturday lunchtime than sit in the local, sipping their drinks and listening to the old master take them back into history.

"Soon after taking his seat, Roger rekindled the old quarrels with the Talbots." Gilbert is in full stride now.

"Because the Rishtons gained their lands from the Talbots when Edmund Talbot was outlawed for debt, this loss of land is a constant smouldering fire in the hearts of future Talbots. Also, on the subject of the Talbots, it was Sir Thomas Talbot, who was a nasty piece of work, that captured King Henry VI at Brungerly Bridge and handed him over to the Yorkies, who took him and put him in the Tower of London. King Henry put a curse on the Talbots that's followed them for nine generations."

"Roger is also involved in many family quarrels, such as the time when he had a dispute with his father-in-law, Henry de Rishton, from the Dunkenhalgh estate."

"Roger claimed that now that he's the lord of the manor of the church, he can sit anywhere he wants during the church service. Henry, on the other hand, as the head of the manor of Dunkenhalgh, thinks that he and *his* family should have the best pews and the best desks to sit in during the service."

"Roger disagreed with this and felt that his status as Lord of the Manor had been undermined, so he decided to take some action one Sunday morning."

Gilbert pauses for a drink, frustrating Ricky and Ralph.

Refreshed, Gilbert prepares to continue. The boys close in. Gilbert gestures. He put some armed men in positions on the four highways that led to the church to stop anyone from Dunkenhalgh from interfering. Later, with some armed rough heads, he forced his way into the church and ripped out the pews put there by Henry, carried them outside and made a bonfire with them in the church yard."

Edgar, meanwhile, gazes at the expressions on the faces of his two sons. Once again, his old dad has the boys right where he wants them. When he tells one of his stories, they are simply putty in his hands. Edgar shakes his head and smiles. He has to admit that he is proud of his father, but he cannot imagine himself ever actually saying so.

"And the worst of all Roger's misdeeds is when he, with three of his cronies, came to Church Kirk and committed an act of sacrilege again, even more scandalous than the first. Armed with various tools and weapons, they destroyed the carved wooden tabernacles of the Virgin Mary and St. Oswald, threw them into the churchyard, and stripped them of all their silver. Then they broke into offertory boxes, stole the contents, and took away the silver chalice that has been in the church since before St. Oswald's time. It was Oswald's monks who built the first wooden Kirk near the holy well that's buried under the east wall of St. James'. Oh, and he also took all ceremonial vestments."

Gilbert took a drink, then added, "And this final act of sacrilege prevented celebration of the Eucharist."

"A Eucharist! What's a Eucharist?" asked Ralph.

Taking advantage of Ralph's interruption, Gilbert drained his glass and ordered another while Edgar briefly explained to his son the need for the chalice during the sacrament of the Lord's Supper. Now lubricated, Gilbert motors serenely on.

"This time Roger is summoned to appear in front of the Lancaster Court of the Privy Seal, where he escaped lightly by being bound to keep the King's peace. And nobody's seen the chalice or vestments since that day." In preparation for his conclusion, stretching his leg out to aid circulation, Gilbert says, "Roger's last battle is with Sir Thomas on Cowhill farm at Rishton, where he is looking to gain revenge on the Talbots. But Sir Thomas heard of Roger's intentions and set a trap for him and his henchmen. Fatally wounded in cut-and-thrust fighting in a yeoman's house, Roger is left for dead. Sir Thomas arrived to see Roger's bleeding body on the kitchen floor, and while a priest is reading him his last rites, Sir Thomas says…"

At this point, Gilbert pauses as if uncertain what is to follow. Running his fingers through his hair, he rehearses the words in his head in order to phrase the quote as accurately as possible. He wonders if he still has his family's attention, but he need not worry. On the edges of their seats, all are keen to hear the conclusion.

"Yes, yes," says Gilbert assuredly. "That's it! Yeah, that's it. Sir Thomas says, and I quote, "Now I will be sure, and I will give unto Rishton my mark." Raising his clenched fist as if holding an imaginary dagger and raising his voice, Gilbert played out the scene. "And with the priest protesting, to be sure his old enemy is dead, Sir Thomas strikes his dagger into the scull of Roger, breaking his weapon with the force of his anger. Triumphantly, he holds the broken bloody dagger high so that his men can see it."

Both boys's mouths are wide open, afraid to move a muscle in case they miss a vital word.

"Sir Thomas says, 'I have sped him. Look, I have broken my dagger in his brains and if my dagger had not broken, I would have used it to strike the priest that tried to prevent me."

Gilbert sits back. Relaxed again, he concludes, "There and then the feud between the Rishtons and the Talbots ended with the violent death of Roger de Rishton."

"Well, what do you think, Ralph? That should make a good essay, eh?" says Gilbert before draining another glass with a flourish. "Yeah," responded Ralph, "that'll be neat."

Chapter 4

July 1962 Part 2

Back in King Georges Hall.

"Richard Rishton," Sir Charles announced.

A final hug from his mother, then under the magnificent Art Deco house lights to a rapturous applause from the adoring local audience, Ricky walks slowly through the orchestra, savouring the atmosphere. Taking a good look around the grandeur of this fine theatre with its original feature plasterwork, he stands beside the immaculate Steinway Grand.

Facing the audience when he bowed, Ricky saw the huge grins of his pals, Dennis 'Harpy' Dawson, sitting with Francis 'Velvet' Wiseman and Raymond 'Redwing' Barron. They are all with their respective girlfriends, Emily Crossley, Susan 'Flash' Gordon and Ethel 'Laughing Water' Mannin. Feeling blue from the lost love of his girlfriend Shirley,

Ricky resigns himself to the fact that she is not coming and turns to sit down with a heavy heart. But unknown to him, no sooner has he turned to face his music than a lone figure appears at an entrance and starts to walk slowly down the centre aisle. Everyone in the auditorium, apart from Ricky, who is lost in concentration on the keyboard, watches each step the brunette takes as she makes her slightly embarrassed way to the front before taking her seat next to her friend, the red-haired Flash.

The embarrassment of seeing his daughter sitting with the common lot, adding to the sight of the ever-growing audience, gives Robert an even redder complexion. Claudette, however, is delighted and, finding it hard to withhold her tears, she hides her face in her handkerchief. Beaming from within, she is so proud of her daughter for showing some independence and standing up for herself at last; for too long, Robert has controlled her life.

Ricky hears the audience mumbling. Curious, he turns and sees Shirley! Delighted and relieved, "Yes, yes," he celebrates.

His warm fingers lingering over the keyboard, his heart full of emotion, Ricky watches Shirley settle into her seat, noticing the new dress she is wearing is made of the same floral-patterned cotton that she wore on the day when they first met.

Chapter 5

Coronation Day, 1953

Shirley

At four o'clock on the morning of June 2nd 1953, Gilbert hoisted the Union flag upon the tower of St. James', ushering in the dawn on what would prove to be a long day for all the inhabitants of Church Kirk.

Eight hours later, the damp felt is glistening on the garage roof and the thin wooden roof and walls vibrate to the sound of the families gathered together inside. Glad to be out of the cold, wet weather, they are singing the Queen's favourite hymn, 'The Lord is my shepherd,' at the top of their voices. Then, standing pole rigid, their shoulders back and heads raised to the blue ceiling, they sing along with the National Anthem, which crackles from the wireless that Mr. Cunliffe, the local electrical shop proprietor, has rigged up. Singing, as if to the sky beyond, their voices rise in volume as they are in fact celebrating the accession to the throne of their newly crowned monarch.

Over several days, Mr. Butts had the cars that were brought in for repair removed. And, to match the colours of the Union Flag, the garage floor was mopped and painted red, the walls whitewashed, and the ceiling painted royal blue. A variety of shapes, sizes and shades of white tablecloths drape over a motley collection of tables, somehow squeezed into every nook and cranny of the gaily-lit garage.

Mr. Butts' garage, the largest covered space available, is situated among others in the grounds of Nelson Square and adjacent to the Sharn Hall lodge. The garage has the benefit of size, situation and an amiable proprietor who, like millions of other citizens of the United Kingdom this day, is determined to make this an occasion to remember for the rest of his life.

Inside, under the muffled drone of an outdoor petrol engine that is connected to a generator to power the electric lights, Mr. Butts and all the other adults follow the Westminster service on the radio.

Reading the order of the service word for word from a copy given free with every copy of the Daily Mirror, they listen to the Coronation.

During the preceding week, each attendant family has cooked and covered the tables with cakes, sandwiches of potted meat, ham, chicken and cucumber, and plates and plates of buns. The children have the choice of jellies of lemon, strawberry, raspberry, blackcurrant, lime, or orange flavour and trifles of all sizes and shapes. The large coronation cake, baked by Mrs. Butts, however, takes pride of place. An ardent royalist, she has shaped the cake into a model of Buckingham Palace, with small marzipan figures of Elizabeth and Philip standing on the roof.

Cooked in the morning, the main meal is roast chicken and Yorkshire pudding, followed by spotted dick and custard. To keep some control over the quantities produced, the children ran from house to house, relaying messages referring to who was cooking what and how much. Mrs. Butts is in charge of the Yorkshire puddings, and Mrs. Halgyth has responsibility for the spotted dick. Mrs. Harp provides the custard, while Mrs. Rishton and Mrs. Talbot were charged with providing the roast chicken and vegetables, respectively. When cooked, the pots, pans and dishes full of hot food are ferried across Nelson Square to the garage at noon and kept warm on Mr. Butts' old Dover stove, which is more commonly used to keep the garage warm during the winter months.

In the garage, Mr. Butts has erected a raised platform with scarcely enough room for a 'Master of Ceremonies' and an upright piano for Ricky to play the anthem.

Due later at two o'clock, when his morning shift at the Thorney Bank coal face has finished, Edgar is to assist with the Tombola.

Both box and wavy streamers coloured red, white and blue hang from the ceiling, and clumps of balloons with ribbons hang from the ceiling. A banner emblazoned with the royal crest and 'God save the Queen' in bold gilded letters adorns the walls, accompanied by pictures of a young Elizabeth. Electric light bulbs of various colours and more bunting, some made from dyed ragbag collections of cast-off clothing, decorate the walls together with brilliantly illuminated E.II.R symbols.

At the garage front, any broken windows have been re-glazed and broken or rotten wallboards mended or replaced before a fresh coat of pale blue paint is applied. Draped over the dried paint, there is more bunting and another Union flag flies from the gold painted finial. Smaller flags protrude up and out of the guttering. Underneath, union pennants droop down from the eves in arches and bannerettes festoon the frontage. The brilliance and cleanliness of all the new colours create an oasis within this desert of dark, dismal streets, houses and factories, typical of so much of East Lancashire.

Inside, the revellers are all seated, chatting with each other. It is an atmosphere of neighbourliness brought about by so many, with so little money, giving so much time to create a perfect day. The noise of their chatter is very nearly as loud as their singing, only abating for a time when great mouthfuls of roast chicken prevent even this garrulous group from talking.

"Stop it!" shouts Mrs. Harp, clipping her son, Douglas, across the ear for flicking her special homemade trifle across the room with his spoon. With so many children beneath one roof, little squabbles are bound to develop, but they die as quickly as they flare up. Crawling under the tables and playing private games of hide and seek or tag captured the youngsters' interest.

****

While everyone else is celebrating in the garage, little Frankie Talbot is climbing up the drainpipe at the back of Edgar's house to gain entry through the first-floor bathroom window.

****

Some of the children are in fancy dresses. There's a cardboard television with a picture of Elizabeth on the screen, which opens on Sellotape hinges, revealing the occupant. There is also a horse, though most have dressed as past Kings and Queens.

Dressing as a page boy doesn't stop Ricky from playing football or competing in a few races across the garage roofs and a couple of circuits on the slide, swings and roundabout in Gatty Park. Seeing him seated at the piano, smiling with his black finger nails and smudged face, Amelia realises she should have dressed him as a scamp.

Dennis Dawson is dressed as a cowboy and is practicing drawing his plastic guns from the two holsters slung low at his hips, firing plastic pellets at his imaginary enemies. Ray Baron is in the full costume of a Native American, adding his personal touch with two feathers hanging from his long black hair. Another friend, the lyrical Ashley Mather, is in more formal attire: a dark blue corduroy suit. Wearing long pants for the first time makes his legs itch. Ricky's elder sister, Edith, while hiding during the game of hide and seek, gets her angels' wings caught between two chairs. She's freed by a giggly dark-skinned girl whom Ray has christened Laughing Water. Attracted to her long black hair, she looks the entire world at him like an Indian squaw.

While food is being consumed, Mrs. Talbot is looking around for Frank, her youngest son and is still looking for him while everyone helps to clear the tables and move them out of the way, stacking them in a far corner to provide floor space.

A row of six chairs is rearranged in front of the platform so that musical chairs can begin.

Ricky is playing Offenbach's 'Can Can,' stopping on every 'C Major', the signal for the contestants to sit. Ray has won his age group and claims his win is due to the advantage of wearing the spiritual combination of Magpie and Jackdaw feathers tied into his hair, but the other kids feel the deft use of a plastic tomahawk on his opponents' heads was the determining factor.

To fill in between the games, Ashley recites Kipling's 'If' all the way through without having to refer to the notes in his pocket should he falter.

After all the children's games are completed, it is time for the Tombola draw, where all the kids receive a prize or memento of the occasion, each worth five shillings.

****

Having fed his skinny body through the narrow gap provided by the open window and catching the foot of his trailing leg in the iron framed window, Frank Talbot hangs upside down. Supporting his weight with both hands on the inside window ledge, he jerks his foot free and falls headfirst into the white cast iron enamelled bath and is knocked unconscious, leaving yet another disfigurement on an already blemished countenance. The window slams, and the clasp snaps shut.

****

As the venerable elder and owner of the venue, Mr. Butts is to present the prizes to the children. Holding up the first coloured ball drawn from a dark blue velvet bag, Edgar, who has just arrived, calls out, "Number twelve."

Clutching his ticket, Dennis Dawson rushes to the platform to claim his prize. When he sees its shape, he instantly knows it is the Hohner Marine ten-hole diatonic harmonica, for which he has been pestering his parents for weeks. Excitedly, almost snatching it, he takes it from Mr. Butts' hand. Eagerly unwrapping his prize, he is blowing and drawing through it enthusiastically, but making an ugly noise while dancing between the tables.

Musician Ricky quickly makes friends with Dennis and helps him understand the music scale. Having a natural ear, Dennis soon gets the hang of it and, for the rest of the day, sits in a corner of the garage, practicing his scales. Subsequently, he is always referred to as Harpy, and from that day onwards, a new friendship develops between him and Ricky as the two embark on contrasting musical careers.

While enjoying giving the presents away, Mr. Butts has a big smile on his face. He is particularly pleased with himself on this day of all days because Edgar has just now paid up on the bet he lost to Mr. Butts concerning the result of the FA Cup Final. Old Butts smiles again as he recalls listening to the match on the radio, being worried when his team, Blackpool, is losing three goals to one to their Lancashire rivals, Bolton Wanderers. But, inspired by Stanley Matthews, Blackpool came back from the dead and Bill Perry scored the winner in the last minute. Unknown to them both on this Coronation Day, Edgar would gain revenge in five days' time when his bet on 'Pinza' in the Derby at 5/1 with the champion jockey, Gordon Richards on board, wins the race. This is the great little jockey's twenty sixth and final attempt to win the blue-ribbon event in the horse racing calendar and the BBC radio news broadcast only the previous day that Richards is to receive a knighthood for his services to the sport.

One of the other two items of news being discussed in the garage this day is the successful ascent of Mt. Everest by the New Zealander, Edmund Hillary and the Nepalese Sherpa, Tenzing Norgay, on May 29th. A few academic members of Church Kirk are commenting on the opening of the Palestinian refugee camp at Jenin in Israel.

Pulling the next number from his bag, Edgar calls, "Four and two, 42." His words are met with a long silence; no one comes to claim the prize. Raising his voice, he repeats the number and the merrymakers check each other's tickets to confirm that none of them have number 42. Surely someone must have it, because he thinks no one has left and Edgar repeats the number a third time. Then he thinks of Mrs. Ridehalgh. Maybe she has it, but she has been rushed away and is in the hospital due to having her firstborn. Unknown to Edgar, she had given birth and, being born on coronation day, the child will receive a £1 pound saving certificate, and a ten-shilling certificate is given to any child born during coronation week.

The anticipation of the whispering crowd is broken when a spoon, licked clean, chinks into a spotless earthenware dish and a scuffling comes from the back row seats. Then the screech of a chair being pushed back in a hidden alcove and like the dawn after a dark night, a young girl coyly edges her way between the tables and stands before Mr. Butts to present her ticket.

Concentrating on playing the introduction, 'Enter the Gladiators', Ricky is unaware of the girl making her way to the platform. As per tradition, he stops while the prize is being handed over, takes a drink of Dandelion and Burdock from his Coronation mug (which every school child received) and looks around to see who's won and what.

That first moment he saw her face, he thought a skilled and cunning master must have drawn her, as on canvas. Her back is held straight to balance the gold painted cardboard crown, trimmed with cotton wool, which sits neatly on her head. She is wearing a knee length crisp cotton floral dress with short sleeves and two pockets at the hips below a narrow elastic waistband. A pure white collar surrounds a slender neck that supports her head, topped with dark curly hair, cut short.

Her slim build disguises a strong frame that carries her with ease. Above a noble little nose, set wide upon her heart shaped face, are two soft blue eyes bright with the wonder of life. With a calm, graceful movement, she holds up her ticket with the regality of the queen she portrays and, trying to rub the scuff marks from the toes of her blue shoes on her white socks, her lips stained red by the raspberry jelly she was scoffing when her number was called, she says, "I am Shirley Talbot; here is number forty-two."

To Ricky, the words came tinkling like rain pelting balloons. Taking her prize from Mr. Butts, the candles in her eyes say, "Thank you."

Unable to remove his gaze, Ricky feels his heart beating heavily from the shock of the pleasure produced by the impact of unexpected beauty. "Shirley Talbot, did she say? I didn't think a Talbot could look like that."

When Shirley gazes at this boy sitting at the piano with his mouth wide open, as one might adore a star, she also feels something, but she doesn't know what. She is simply enchanted by his playing and charmed by his smile. Later, they share the piano stool and while their parents tidy up the garage after everyone else has gone home, they spend what is to her a magical hour. Blissfully enveloped in their own play, they are completely unaware of the incongruity of them sitting on the tiny stage in the garish red, white and blue setting; each feeling a sense that they are bound to one another.

The festivities are over, and the Rishton family waits patiently behind Edgar while he searches his pockets for the front door key. While he fumbles, Amelia, Ralph, Edith, and Ricky stand back to admire the display their next-door neighbour, Mr. Ward, has spent over a month making. He is the winner of the prize for the best house decorated in the street during Coronation Week. There are thirty-eight large flags, over eighty small ones, a window centre piece of orb, mace, sceptre, ampulla, ring and other coronation regalia, all made from wood by Mr. Ward, a joiner by trade. There is also a 'throne' with crown and other emblems and lettering. At night, coloured lights illuminate the whole display.

Amelia moves forward and, just testing, pushes on the door. It opens. Realising the door must have been 'unlocked' all day, she turns to Edgar and raises her eyebrows. His bladder bursting, Ricky runs up the stairs to the bathroom. Lifting the toilet seat, he stands there in blissful relief, unaware of the presence of others. The tiny hairs on the back of his neck stand up when he hears a groan echo off the white bathroom tiles. Whizzing his head around, he sees Frankie's dazed, ugly features rise out of the bath.

His stream cut short; Ricky calls out. "Dad! Dad!"

"What? What?" Edgar calls back.

"There's a strange boy in our bath," Ricky shouts, buttoning his fly.

In seconds, Edgar appears at the door and sees his son wrestling with the boy on the bathroom floor. Breaking them apart, he holds on to the back of the strange boy's ragged yellow and green checked jumper.

Edgar questions the frightened youth. "What are you doing in here? How did you get in here? And who are you?"

The boy just looks at the floor, saying nothing. Normally kept open, Ricky notices the closed bathroom window. He says, 'There! Through there, I'll bet," pointing to how he might have gained entry.

The boy raises and turns his head to Ricky and gives him an evil, vengeful look. Edgar marches him down the stairs, along the lobby, to the front door. Intending to merely throw him out and leave the incident at that, he thinks the fright of discovery might be sufficient punishment. Meanwhile, the youngest Rishton, Edgar's daughter Jean, stops opening her coronation present and shouts from the living room, 'He's one of them Talbots, Frank his name is, but I think they call him Scrine. Look at him, ugly git."

A Talbot, hey, thinks Edgar for a moment, then frog marches 'Scrine' back to his parents' house three streets away and tells them where he found him and to sort him out. "But if there's a next time, I'll take him straight to the police station," promises Edgar.

Chapter 6

July 1962 Part 3

Ricky Plays

As Shirley takes her seat on the front row, Ricky cannot help feeling that nine years on, she has grown even more beautiful and he's more in love with her now than on that first day of the reign of Queen Elizabeth II.

Looking at her sitting there, her eyes radiantly smiling back at him, Ricky is suddenly conscious of her growing womanhood, and as he too is growing up, the words from a verse of a Shelley poem, 'She moves upon this earth a shape of brightness,' ** came to mind.

Giving her a welcoming smile, "I'll bet Shelley had fewer problems writing that piece than I've had convincing my dad there is some good in a Talbot," Ricky thinks to himself.

A bright girl, Shirley graduated from Oswaldtwistle High School for Girls with seven 'A' levels. While she decides whether to try for a place at university, she's working for her father, Robert Talbot, the owner and managing director of Talbot Furniture Stores in Accrington. Her side of the Talbot family has become quite affluent and is therefore able to pay for her to have music lessons. Under Ricky's influence, she has developed into a proficient musician and after trying all kinds of instruments, she's finally settled on the violin. She and Ricky play duets on special civic occasions, and knowing Robert would never set foot in working men's clubs, they sometimes play as a trio in the local clubs with Harpy. That, however, was before Ricky went on to study in Manchester. Feeling 'Church Kirkish' for a moment, he thinks 'to hell with convention' and gives his friends a double thumbs up, which they return in unison.

A smiling Harpy raises his harmonica, a cheeky signal to Ricky that he is ready to take over the music should he forget the notes. He and Ricky had continued to practice together before Ricky left for Manchester College. Ricky looked back at his friend and smiled in wry agreement. All right, mate, he nodded. Then, still thinking of his 'golden dream', he takes his seat at the piano. Making adjustments to his seat to accommodate his height, he looks up and nods to the conductor, saying that he is ready to begin. Sir Charles Groves raises his baton, the audience hush and the orchestra begins.

Suffocating, Ricky loosens his bowtie and unbuttons his collar. 'Ah, that's better,' he thinks. With crooked fingers, he places his well-practiced hands over the ivory keyboard and begins to play the introduction before moving on to the first variation of the rhapsody.

He plays on to that lusciously romantic variation number 18, which is nearly a piano solo, playing with remarkable feeling for someone so young. Running through an extraordinary gamut of emotions, Ricky keeps his audience bewitched.

Robert was expecting an ordeal and he sits motionless throughout, but inside his considerable bulk, affected by the atmosphere in the auditorium and induced by the live performance of Rachmaninov's composition executed by Ricky and the RLPO, he is taken on an emotional roller coaster. Before tonight, he would never have believed it possible. The anxiety of years building his business and struggling to be the top dog pours from his rediscovered soul and tears of emotion run down his fat cheeks. Is his heart finally softening? So engrossed in the music, Robert has not noticed the auditorium is full to capacity.

After fourteen minutes of playing, Ricky comes to the last variation, number 24, which ends unexpectedly with a few gentle notes. On the last note, which he executes with a perfect touch, the audience erupts into a crash of applause. Then their massed attention focuses on Robert, who is out of his seat, clapping vigorously. There was no sign of any disappointment to be seen by the assembled masses. The Reverend and Gilbert have also noticed the full house and passed each other satisfied glances.

Ricky rises from his stool, turns to the audience and bows. Wiping his brow with the loose end of his black silk bowtie, he moves to the side to shake the hand of the leader of the orchestra, then walks to the conductor's podium and shakes the hand of Sir Charles.

As he does so, Ricky sees his mother in the wings, miming for him to do up his tie but smiling broadly with pride. Ricky takes another bow before walking to the wings and into the arms of his mother. Shortly after, he returns to the stage for an encore, shakes the hands of the conductor and lead violinist again, before finally, after four encores, he turns to face the audience. Bowing deeply, his face touching his kneecaps, his nose catches the whiff of St. Bruno. Rising slowly, he looks into the audience, searching for his granddad's flat cap. Spotting the Labour Party's red badge on its neb, he also notices his father is sitting beside the old man. Standing straight, Ricky raises his hand and eagerly waves to them both. To his right, his eye catches Mrs. Talbot wagging her finger at Robert.

"Now, can't you see what a wonderful future son-in-law you could have?" remonstrated Claudette. Sheepishly, Robert, seeing the audience's standing ovation, has to admit there must be something in this music business after all. Yet, smoothing his blue tie, he still tries to calculate the takings at the door in his head.

In the wings of the hall during the intermission, Ricky is delighted to be reunited with Shirley. Not having to return to the piano for a couple of hours to begin the next piece, the 'Overture Solennelle 1812 op 49', he goes to his dressing room, sits down and smiles. The sight of his three friends 'dressed up' has illuminated a day from their past—one of the four's great adventures and their wonderful discoveries.

Chapter 7

November 1st 1957, Part 1

The Gathering.

It's 7 o'clock in the morning, and the first light has begun to open this extraordinary day when Velvet, Redwing, Harpy and Ricky meet by the St James' Churchyard gateway before they head down the Dunk. Virtually encircled by the Leeds and Liverpool canal, 'the Dunk' is a wonderful area of  vegetation. It is full of wild life and populated by stout native trees in the woods around a majestic Elizabethan manor house, the centrepiece of Dunkenhalgh Park. Finding such a wonderful natural playground this close to the industrial smoke-filled squalor of Accrington and Oswaldtwistle is a paradise for our adventure-seeking youngsters. A mental map of the Dunk is etched into the boys' brains; they know all of its secrets and hiding places. The possessors of not much money but lots of imagination, it's their whole world throughout the school holidays, after school and at week-ends (homework permitting), and they're out from morning until dusk. Only sickness will keep them indoors. By now, they are due to leave school and the world of work is beckoning. New habits such as smoking, drinking and girls are beginning to take priority, but on a fine Saturday morning with the whole of the day in front of them, there is only one place to go, and that is down the Dunk.

The air is still and a sweet scent from Wm. Blyth's chemical works hangs in the early morning mist as the first to arrive, Velvet, sits down at the entrance to the churchyard.

Pushing forward his legs, he leans his shoulder on the right sandstone pillar that once supported the old iron gates. Gently and a little nervously, a proud and optimistic Velvet removes from a filthy cotton bag his new ferret and lovingly strokes it. He's paid the princely sum of two shillings and sixpence—two weeks paper round money—with promises that it is 'a good un'.

While trying to think of a name for the new member of the ratting team, he removes an oblong tin from the top pocket of his green combat jacket, which contains his Golden Virginia tobacco and Rizla cigarette papers. He peals a paper from the pack and fills it with GV.

His slim dog, Tan, an elegant bitch whippet, owes her name to the colour of her coat. She sits next to him, sniffing at the latest member of the family. With no name for the ferret coming immediately to mind, Velvet knows he will simply have to wait and be patient. He licks the hand-rolled cigarette paper. "Anyway," he says to himself, "most names evolve from some event or are given because of some particular characteristic like a spot on the tail or a patch on the eye." But there are no distinguishing features on this pink-eyed albino; it's pure Surf White. Lighting up his crinkled roll-up with a match he keeps loose in the tobacco tin, he takes a long drag and pouts a blue ring into the mist. He thinks of Snowy, or, in contrast, Blacky, or maybe just Black, so, with his dog, he can have Black and Tan. "But na," he thinks, "that's too easy and common." He decides to dwell on it another day unless something inspires him or provokes his imagination.

He begins reciting a poem in his head when, all of a sudden, the ferret, for no apparent reason, bites his hand. Blood rushed to his head, his light brown voice turning dark. "Bastard," the 'Velvet fog' cursed. He grabs the ferret and roughly stuffs it back in the bag.

Velvet, the tallest and oldest of the four, is a man of a strange temperament with a mild demeanour and savage moods. He has a permanent grin on his long face and a determined jaw. When angered, though, he doesn't rant and rave as the others might, but he expresses his anger through action. Most alarmingly, no one can predict when, until the action is in progress or is over.

With both his parents being teachers, he is regarded as coming from 'a good family'.

Even on hunting days, Velvet remains clean and tidy. Redwing once noted that he has never had holes in his socks. Why he considers holes in socks to be the normal state of dress is possibly a testament to his own upbringing. But they all know Velvet is not afraid of getting 'stuck in' when any dirty work is required, and for this, he has their respect.

It is a bit cold this autumn morning; at least until the sun breaks through and so Velvet is wearing a warm green combat jacket, Levi jeans and Wellington boots. There is, however, no protection for his head. Not wanting to crease his wavy hair, which is always neatly combed straight back off his brow, he never wears a cap. A green silk cravat, tied loosely around his neck, protects his vocal cords. From his good school education, he's gained an understanding of Latin and, blessed with excellent recall, relishes any opportunity to recite one of his many memorised poems.

****

After getting dressed in the blue-black cold, his young eyes keen enough to find his way in the dark, Ricky rushes downstairs, through the living room and opens the kitchen door. Switching on the light, he hears the familiar sound of cockroaches scurrying across the floor. He is always amazed at the speed at which they move. Only once has he managed to see one when it bulked in the queue to hide in the nearest scar in the linoleum. Ignoring them, Ricky fills the whistle kettle with water, strikes a Swan Vesta to light the gas ring and places the copper-bottomed kettle over the heat.

About five minutes after Velvet had lit his roll-up, Raymond Baron emerged from the mist and with his long black hair, black eyes and facial features, you could imagine that you were looking at an Apache, Cherokee, or Commanche.

Ray has always dreamt of being a Native American Indian. His interest began when he read the book 'Grey Owl' by Archibald Belaney, borrowed from the Church Kirk library, a small single-story red brick building.

Indians wear feathers in their hair to show how brave a warrior they have been in battle. Likewise, Ray wears two feathers hanging behind his right ear. Removed from birds he's caught, he took just one tail feather and to follow Indian tradition, he thanked the bird for its gift before releasing it. One feather is from a Magpie, and as is required by an Indian warrior, he has split the feather two-thirds down the quill to signify that he's been wounded. In his case, he has been bitten by rats many times! The other feather is from a Raven. He chose this bird because he once heard Velvet recite the Edgar Allan Poe poem of the same name. He's cut a small wedge out of the right side of the raven's feather to show that he's killed an enemy, in his case, 'a rat or a rabbit,' or that he has taken a scalp 'skinned the rabbit'. Both feathers are tied into his long, straight black hair with a thin leather bootlace.

The imaginative Velvet has christened him 'Redwing.'

Redwing's left elbow sticks out like he's carrying something invisible. It doesn't bother him; in fact, he's learned that the natural gap between his body and elbow is just right for him to rest his 410-gauge shotgun, or the long club he favours, under his arm when he hooks his thumbs in the belt tab of his jeans.

A Woodbine wobbling between his thin lips, Redwing greets Velvet with a characteristic open left palm raised to the shoulder, and like a crow, he croaks, "How!"

Contrary to Velvet's more conservative outlook on life, Redwing is his own man who lives in his own world. Brought up on the land by his gamekeeper father, he has developed a great interest in all things to do with the countryside. His outdoor life has also ensured he sustains a red-weathered complexion. Seduced by adverts for 'Wild Woodbine, the great little cigarette', the 'Wild' in the advert appeals to his concept of the Dunkenhalgh with its unfenced wildness, and he smokes nothing else unless it's free. Not having the musical or literary talents of his three friends, he intends to follow his father and become a gamekeeper and he has secured a position on an estate in the Trough of Bowland after he completes his general education at Rhyddings School, Oswaldtwistle.

His black hair falling over his shoulders, Redwing sits down cross-legged on the stone step beside the scholar. He is not quite as tall as Velvet and is thinner; he is, in fact, all skin and bone. Always, no matter what the weather or season, he wears his shirt unbuttoned to his waist, exposing his inverted chest to the elements. To show off his sinewy, heavily tattooed arms, he rolls his red check cotton shirtsleeves right up to his armpits. On the inside of his left wrist, to ensure that his spirit leaves his body unhindered when he dies, he wears the tattoo of a Umane, which is an oblong with a slightly tapered line out from each north, south, east and west corner, with no sharp corners. Due to the combination of heavy smoking and all-weather chest exposure, he has developed a wonderful cough that arrives in a low-octave A-flat major when prompted by his first drag on a newly lit cigarette.

He holds his jeans up with a brown leather belt, clasped with a large bronze buckle in the shape of an Indian chief's head, the war bonnet brilliant in colourful enamel. A bowie knife, slung to the left, hangs from his belt. His preferred footwear is, of course, the moccasin, but when out hunting, as he is today, he wears boots with steel toecaps for kicking rats. With him is his muscular dog, a smooth-coated beige Lurcher called Buck.

Buck is a hard dog and carries many facial scars caused by his frequent fighting. A large part of his left ear is missing from when he once had the audacity to take on Sean, the top dog in Church Kirk. This piece of absent flesh gives his head a lopsided, comical look, which belies his formidable courage. Redwing's final accessory this morning is his bald (barkless) club-come walking stick. He holds it across his knees when he sits cross-legged on the stone step.

****

While he waits for the kettle to boil, Ricky starts to beat the fire. Removing the spent grey ashes from the fire grate, he screws up some newspaper and stuffs it into the grate, adding some wood before he then puts coal on top of the wood. He spreads a full sheet of the Evening Telegraph across the front of the fireplace to draw air through the grill. Then, with a spill, he lights the print beneath the grate. While kneeling to check that the fire is taking hold, he hears the kettle blow and goes back into the kitchen to pour the boiling water over Lipton's loose tea leaves. Leaving the tea to brew, he saws two thick slices off the two-pound farmhouse loaf and shoves them under the high grill. He's learned from past experiences that eating some breakfast is essential to stave off weakness, especially should the hunt last all day, so he drops an egg in a pan of boiling water.

After a few minutes, Harpy steps forward. "I think Bert's not coming," he says, licking dried pink toothpaste from the corner of his mouth. "He must have a bad cold cos he's been flobbing oysters all night. I nearly slipped on my ass," pointing back in the general direction of Bert's house with his thumb, "flags are full of snot outside his window."

Harpy, shorter than the other two, has a pleasant, angelic face with a smooth, fresh complexion. His hair is brown, uncombed and stuffed under a black beret. A heavy hand-knitted green pullover, with one deep pocket on the front to house his harmonica, covers the well-muscled torso he's gained from swimming. Attending the same St. Christopher's School as Ricky, he is a member of the swimming team. And using his agricultural crawl stroke, he's won several trophies, but it is feared that his lack of height will hamper his progress.

His ability to produce instant music on his harmonica makes him popular with the girls.

During the weekly school dance and music lessons, as soon as the class teacher gives the word to choose a partner, Harpy races across the assembly hall to choose the same girl as always. He believes Emily Crossley to be the best-looking girl in school and they dance well together, seeming to blend into a single movement during the waltzes. Because of the looseness of the movement and rhythm, they enjoy the barn dance the most. Never being shy with girls, he asked Emily out, and within the first week, he saw her on the school playground. He found from her friends her favourite song, practiced it and one morning at break time, on one knee, he serenaded her with the Brahms Cradle song as she sat on the cemetery wall with Pendle Hill in the background and a stream of white steam from Huncoat power station cooling towers pouring elegantly into a clear blue sky. How could she refuse the offer to go and see Victor Mature and Anita Ekberg in 'Zarak' at the Oswaldtwistle Palladium? They dance every week and go out on occasions, but no serious dating has matured while they are still at school.

Gunmetal blue industrial jeans, the ones with large back pockets and white stitching, cover his lower half. Wellies turned down to the instep in the style of a pirate to protect his feet. As Redwing does, he carries a bowie knife strapped to his belt; he has also brought a double-barrelled 12-bore shotgun, cocked under his arm. He also has with him his bitch Judy, another beige Lurcher. She's smaller, with a darker sandy coat than Buck, and she has a white blaze between her eyes. Following behind them is his other dog, 'Bon Appetit," a little black smooth-haired Jack Russell with a brown and black patch over either eye. Holding his head high, Bon carries an expression of a cheery demeanour that gives the impression he's whistling as he scuttles along on four thumbs.

Two Domino cigarettes, one tucked behind each ear, bought at the corner shop along with two matches at the cost of tuppence, complete Harpy's accoutrements.

The three patiently wait for Ricky, saying very little this early in the morning.

Ricky

With the fire successfully beaten, a hurrying Ricky shuts the back door with his foot. Lips tightly closed and cheeks swollen with oats and tea, with one woolly-gloved hand still holding a slab of toast while his other hand is trying to hold on to the lead of his eager bitch, Beauty. Ricky is the last to spirit through the mist.

At his heels is Beauty, a black, shiny, shaggy-coated Jack Russell who has large black eyes and long lashes that give her film star looks. Ricky thinks she should be called Betty after the famous actress, Bette Davis.

"Sorry, I'm late," he apologises to his three friends. "I slept in a bit."

Because it isn't easy for him to regularly meet up with his mates and the dogs, he relishes every opportunity. As long as he fits in his piano practice, he always looks to be out hunting, fishing, 'conkering', nesting, raiding the Dunkenhalgh orchard when the fruit is ripe, or flying through the air on a tree rope swing. They revel in the exhilaration of the chase when they run through the river as a posse in pursuit of rats. They splash through the cold and murky water of the river 'Stink', so called because of the twice-daily discharges from the upstream sewage works. The Stink emerges from a tunnel with clumps of white foam floating on the surface; folklore swears it is 'rat spit'!!

They throw stones, they shout, they curse and the dogs will be up front chasing, barking and yelping, all in the thrill of the chase. Although he knows his mother will be furious with him, like the time he used a brand-new blazer to beat out a grass fire, he will neglect the need to protect his hands and join in the dig, where they use rough sticks that scratch and graze the skin off his fingers, cause blood blisters, or strain his fingers prising and lifting stones. When she sees the dirt wedged under his finger nails, Amelia knows he's been up to no good despite all his excuses. But a few scratches on

41

his hands are a small price to pay for the joy of being in the thick of the hunt and a welcome escape from the labour of practice.

He's a skinny lad and his hair is curled up where it rests on his collar. On this chilly morning, he has chosen to wear his thick black corduroy-hunting jacket, which has two breast and side pockets with red overhanging flaps. The pockets have white pleats in the centre that match the white lapels and ivory buttons fastened with corded loops. On each lapel is a cream plastic ferret. He's fond of the jacket because it's warm and has two large inside pockets, the left one for a ferret and the right for his stock of coltsfoot rock he always buys from Muriel's toffee shop across the road from his house. Well-worn when he found it on the local council tip whilst searching for bicycle parts, the jacket's left side pocket is ripped down one seam, and its red lining hangs like a dog's tongue. After having used it for beating out fires and been trodden on when digging out rat holes, it is, to put it mildly, in a poor condition. He's wearing a red and white herringbone neckerchief and blue jeans, patently ripped at the knees and pockmarked with holes made by battery acid leakage.

To some in more modern times, ripped jeans may be a fashion statement, but to Ricky, the rips are the scars of battle, each with a tale to tell of some great ratting expedition. And as long as they cover his ass, it's ok to wear them. Wellies turned over from the top to stop chafing behind his knees and keep his feet dry. Up at the summit is a khaki-coloured bush hat that matches the tidemark around his neck. He shapes the hat's brim the best he can into a 'John Wayne' Stetson.

Chapter 8

November 1957, Part 2

The Hunt

Having checked for all the pre-requisites for a successful hunting trip, cigarettes, matches, chewing gum and coltsfoot rock, Velvet decides it is time to get started.

Like the actor Ward Bond summoning his wagon train forward, with a slow exaggerated sweep of a straight left arm, he announces as if to the whole of East Lancashire …
"Hey up! Let's go o o o."

Dogs on their leads, the hunting party (four boys, five dogs and a ferret) set off down the dry St. James's tarmacadam road.

Busy fishing for a stick of coltsfoot rock in his inside pocket, Ricky drops Beauty's lead. Immediately she bolts towards the chicken farm gate.

"Hey, Beauty, she off!" screeches Ricky.

Her black leather lead trailing, Beauty squeezes under the bottom bar of the five-barred gate. "She must be on to something," says Redwing.

"Shit, I'd better go find her," says Ricky.

Keeping their dogs held on tight leads, the others make their way towards the farm. The farm looks deserted and there is no sign of Beauty. Figuring the farmer must be away, they lift their dogs over the padlocked gate and climb over themselves.

It is an uncomfortable feeling being there because the farmer has made it clear on many occasions that he doesn't want them on his land. They know they would be in deep trouble should he return but nevertheless, the lads march across the concrete yard and passing the rows of sheds, the hundreds of caged chickens create one hell of a racket. Pulling hard on his lead, Buck leads them down to the bottom of the yard.

"There, she's there," shouts Harpy.

"Here, hold these," he says. And handing Velvet his dog leads, he sets off running down the yard to where Beauty is stood barking at a rat that's crossing over a desolate flat acre of crust capped chicken shit. Not thinking why Beauty has stopped and will go no further, Harpy runs straight past her.

The rat has stopped on a green island some yards away and is looking back at Harpy as if to goad him forward. A supercharged Harpy takes the bait and is halfway across when his weight breaks the thin crust of chicken shit. His wellies start to sink.... fast. Trapped and sinking, Harpy can only watch as the rat jogs away.

"You pillock," says Velvet.

"Ha, ha, ah, pluck, pluck, pluck," says Redwing.

"I'm sure I saw rat laughing." says Ricky.

Now they know the crust is too thin to bear their weight, they are not going over the crust. But Harpy needs help so Velvet searches for something to pull him out with.

Harpy is sinking, too quickly he is up to his waist. A rope is holding some bins together. Ricky unties the rope and throws it out towards Harpy. He grabs and holds it while they heave him out of the stinking pit.

"You stink," says Velvet.

"I can't go home like this," Harpy says, covered in muck.

"Jump in the canal," says Redwing.

"Aye, it'll wash all shit off," says Ricky.

Without hesitation, Harpy jumps. "You'd better get off home now and get changed," says Velvet.

Embarrassed, Harpy squelches his way down the lane, but is determined to return.

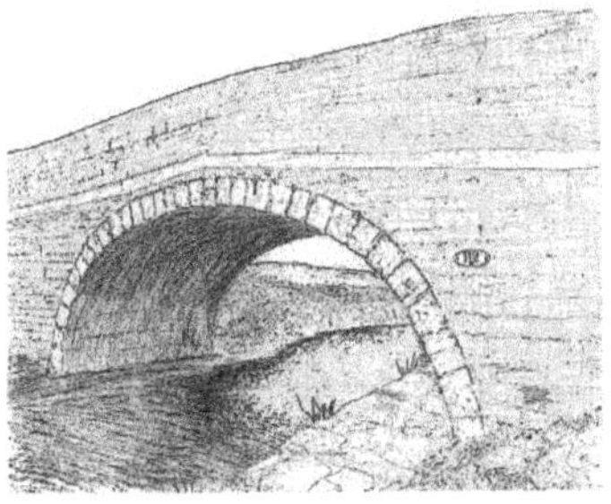

Walking down St. James Road, the reduced hunting party makes their way towards the gateway to adventure, the solid stone-built Bridge Number 112, 'in picture,' which straddles the Leeds and Liverpool canal. As they approach, after the confines of the terraced houses, they're greeted with a wide blue sky. Pausing on the hump, further colour where wild and wide mingle every green of grass and leaf—the fields and woods, with the freedom to safely roam.

Lower, to the left, sits farmer Thornley's mansion-like house. The dirt path then descends steeply. Should you have taken this route, you'd pass by a collection of allotments where flowers and vegetables were grown and poultry and rabbits were bred for the table. At the bottom were ex-filter beds, which were flat, hard, and green, ideal for playing football or cricket, and a brook where a heron fed on silver sticklebacks and water voles that built their nests in the banks. The brook then disappeared into a round tunnel, which you could walk through to get to another wild playground. The path then rose steeply up to the canal and Mattison's farm and fields, where the marsh-loving snipe bred and the sky-loving buzzard hovered. And higher still, across the canal and railway line, is the well-manicured golf course, with its party of greens meeting the blue horizon. Gone now!

With this panoramic view before them, they drink in the crisp morning air and turn right. Without a fence to stop them, they step onto the black dirt path and release the dogs from their leads. Leaving the mist-covered, long, winding industrial waterway behind, the intrepid ratters follow the hawthorn-hedged path, passing Henderson's farm,

'Ponthalgh,' where the trees, barn, and sheds are all quiet. Looking to the left, almost hidden among trees and bushes, are the silent, peaceful buildings of Mattison's farm, gleaming white, its gardens full of autumn colours, and where a glinting gold house barge meanders afloat the hidden Leeds-Liverpool canal, and above, dark green, a busy steam train whistles a salute to the barge as it rushes by in the opposite direction, and with its greeting over, it vanishes.

Now! It's down, down into the beautiful wildness, a route that each has travelled many times and as always, none fail to feel the excitement that accompanies each buoyant step; the hunt is on!

Down the old-rutted lane, worn deep by generations of pilgrims, merchants and, like the lads, adventurers. To the right is a hedgerow of hawthorn and blackthorn, their branches clustered with berries, stark crimson against green leaves and the grasses that tickle their feet. Below the hedge, the dog-rose hips are scarlet and the fruit of the scrambling bramble is purple and black. To the left is a red 'Nori' brick ruin of an old mill with its two pools, which, though the spring and summer flowers are all gone, are a haven for frogs, newts and sticklebacks.

Sloping up and away are rich green fields where black and white cows graze, indifferent to the hunting party.

Through the woods, the splendid Dunkenhalgh manor house can be seen, but nearer there's the derelict watchtower that looks over the stone bridge that Roger de Rishton destroyed many years ago.

The rebuilt bridge straddles a stream that runs into the river Hyndburn and is the same bridge over which the ghost of a 'White Lady', allegedly the sister of Sir John Southworth of Samlesbury, Lady Dorothe, is reputed to ride over on New Year's Eve.

In 1542, when she was only fifteen years old, she married John Rishton of Dunkenhalgh, son of Henry Rishton. Upon their divorce in 1556, part of the divorce settlement may have involved a lifetime tenure: that the manor of Holte in Rishton should revert to Roger de Rishton of Ponthalgh after Dorothe's death. How Dorothe became the White Lady of the Bridge when the legend suggests she is also the White Lady of Samlesbury is unclear, since she probably lived and died in Samlesbury Hall. *

The boys head down to the river and set the dogs away to sniff through the dewy net of gossamer.

Then, in the copse ahead, Beauty starts yapping. She's marking a hole below a hawthorn tree. The tree, bent by the prevailing wind and carrying a rich harvest of berries, sits above the riverbank near the fork where the river Hyndburn meets Hyndburn Brook.

Her tail wagging is a guide to the hole. She yelps as she digs until Buck shoulders her out of the way. The power of his digging has the hawthorn shaking, littering the ground with its red fruit and already he is up to his shoulders in the soft topsoil.

Realising his chance to blood his ferret has arrived, Velvet moves forward and takes the 'virgin' ferret out of its bag. The others, well-schooled in ratting tactics, move their dogs to a position where they can chase down anything that might bolt.

Redwing pulls Buck out of the way, Velvet kneels down, leans forward, lays his free hand on the ground and gently releases the ferret at the mouth of the excavated hole.

In the rust-coloured undergrowth, free from the darkness of the stinking cotton bag, her pink eyes blink in the bright light. Her cherry snout sniffs the sweet country air and her brush tail stiffens at the scent of the resident rodent down deep within. Guided by her primitive instincts to a fate unknown, her sleek body taut, her tense white whiskers brushing the dark clay walls of the foreboding labyrinth, the white assassin moves slowly, cautiously, down.

Tension builds—anticipation of a chase; what will bolt, a rat or a rabbit? And from which of the many escape holes? The dogs start whining with excitement and the boys struggle to hold them still.

Then it is as if every living thing has stopped; is poised, waiting, an eerie calm inhabiting the copse. The boys are holding their breath, there's and the dogs' eyes are scanning the ground.

Sat cross-legged opposite one of the escape holes, Redwing holds a soiled Buck tight. Trembling in expectation, Buck's red wet tongue hangs, long stalactites of saliva streaming from his panting mouth. To test his theory that rats are not scared of ferrets, but can be enticed out of their hole by the aroma of a Woodbine, Redwing uses his free hand to calmly light 'Britain's most popular cigarette'.

The others hold their ground, watching.

Redwing's falcon eyes spot movement to his left, "There!" he shouts.

Buck breaks free and is quick in pursuit. With his club at the ready, Redwing follows him, smiling at his timing; then another rat bolts from a blind hole.

"There, another one!" calls Ricky, springing into action. He runs after Beauty as she chases the rat down towards the river.

While his pals are busy in their pursuits, Velvet sits with Tan beside the hole, watching and waiting for his ferret to come out.

Judy soon caught up with the first rat to bolt and a tug of war starts when Bon arrives and grabs the back end of the rat; stripping off its skin. Both dogs spring apart worrying their share of the prey.

Buck is barking up a terracotta pipe, so Redwing has lost his prey. Disgusted both turn away and head for the river where they hear Ricky shouting and Beauty yapping. From the bank, Ricky throws his last stone at a rat swimming upstream towards the sewage works.

Needing to reassert his reputation as the best hunter. Without hesitation, Redwing runs straight into the black water, stilled by the depth. Wading-in up to his waist, the cold causes a sharp intake of breath. With deep gulps of air, holding his club in both hands above his head for balance, his feet slipping sometimes on the stony bottom, he edges forward.

Behind Redwing, swimming hard, Buck soon catches up with, Beauty paddling frantically.

From the bank, "Go on, Beauty!" Ricky shouts.

"Come on, Buck! Get in there."

"Come on Redwing, it's getting away," Ricky urges.

"I'm fucking trying," says Redwing, feeling his way cautiously, struggling to negotiate the uneven riverbed.

In front of Redwing, Beauty is swallowing water and Buck's barks have turned to gurgles.

With its streamlined body, waterproof fur coat and webbed feet, the rat is well adapted to this environment. Its back just under the water line, only its pinned back ears, black snout and black beady eyes can be seen above the water line. Skimming through the water, confident in reaching its hide hole in the far bank, its eyes sparkle in the sunlight as if it is enjoying the chase.

Shy of the water, Judy and Bon stay on the bank, lending their support by barking and leaping in the air. Meanwhile Velvet is getting increasingly frustrated, constantly looking over his shoulder trying to watch the chase yet knowing he has to keep an eye out for his ferret in case it comes out and is lost in the scrub.

Redwing notices the rat is starting to tire and the twinkle in its eyes has dulled. Heading for the far bank, it is visibly slowing and Buck is only about a yard behind, his strong shoulders driving him on as he's closing in.

"Now!" shouts Redwing, "now Buck, Now!"

Buck raises his head up out of the water to open his jaws. Thrusting forward, he snaps them shut.

'Plop', the rat disappears.

Confused at the sudden vanishing, Buck starts to tread water. And in disarray, he spins in circles. Unaware from her water line view of what has happened, Beauty's little legs keep paddling forward. Franticly struggling to hold her head up she bumps into Buck. Tired, she ducks under the water.

"Buck! Get Beauty," Redwing shouts.

"Beauty! Beauty!" Ricky calls.

Buck ducks his head underwater, but comes up with nothing.

"She's fucked," says Redwing.

Buck dives again; his whole-body disappearing.

Time passes. Buck has been under the water a long time and Redwing starts to worry. Ricky throws his club to one side and starts to take his boots off—ready to wade in.

Then Buck's black nose breaks the surface, then his front paws and between his jaws, held by the scruff of her neck, a sodden Beauty. She coughs once and her dignity infringed, she starts barking, demanding to be released.

"Yeeeeah!" All three shout and throw a welly into the air.

"Drop her," shouts Redwing.

Buck lets go. Redwing grabs her by the scruff of the neck and carries her to the bank.

"Ok, so where did the rat fuck off to?" Redwing asks as his Indian eyes scan the river.

"I don't know, but it is a fucking big un," says the newly arrived Harpy.

"Hey up! lad," the others greeted him.

"I'll bet it's dived and it's swimming for an underwater hidey hole," says Redwing. And pointing directly in front, he wades steadily ahead. "That's where I'm heading anyway, straight on," he says.

His gun held at the ready, "I'll watch for it from this side," says Harpy,

"Right, I'll head for yonder bank," says Ricky and makes a move for the same bank Redwing is heading for.

Arriving together, Ricky holds out a stick for his pal to grab a hold of to pull him out. Redwing though, can't pull his boots out of the mud. He pulls harder, but being stronger than Ricky, he pulls him off balance.

Feeling himself falling, Ricky lets go of the stick and grabs hold of an overhanging branch; gripping hard to prevent himself from falling backwards. But he slips on the wet-bank and slides down. Luckily though, only his wellies enter the river.

Redwing starts laughing. And relieved he hadn't fallen in full length, "fucking hell, that were close", says Ricky.

Harpy is laughing from the far bank and shouts, "Hey Redwing! Make for the shallow end, up there," and points to the rough line of stone above the water line, but Redwing has another idea.

While Ricky scrambles up the bank, Redwing pulls one foot out of its boot then reaches down into the river, pulls the boot free and throws it onto the bank; repeating the same with the other foot. Then, grabbing the same overhanging branch as Ricky used, he starts pulls himself out.

"There! Redwing…the rat's right by your side," shouts Ricky.

"It's trying to get down your collar." says Harpy.

Redwing looks down. There, right next to his elbow, its whiskers splayed like a fan across the skin of white scum, the rat's nose and startled eyes stare up at him. For a moment, they look into each other's eyes.

"Fucking bastard!" Redwing shrieks and lashes out with his fist.

"Fuckin' hell!" He curses, loses his grip and slips back into the river.

Scared by the encounter, plop! The rat dives again.

While Redwing pulls himself out 'again,' Harpy scans the surface of the river for the rat.

Sitting on the bank together, Ricky and Redwing, empty their wellies and ring out their socks before hurrying to pull them back on.

Near them, straight from the river, Buck and Beauty shake their coats, spraying the two ratters with cold water.

"What the fuck?" Ricky shouts, holding up his arm against the shower.

"Get out of it!" Redwing shoves Buck away.

His keen brown eyes spot the rat swimming up the river. Buck starts barking and sets off in hot pursuit, with Beauty following.

Not having been in the thick of the action, Velvet has become even more agitated, constantly looking around to see what is happening, but still keeping one eye on the hole should a rat or his ferret emerge.

Swimming towards a rotten tree trunk half submerged, the rat leaves behind wedge-shaped ripples on the water's surface.

Redwing watches, he knows there is an escape route there, because many a hunt has come to an end just there.

He makes straight for the log. Ricky and Harpy catch up. And, swimming hard, Buck is gaining.

Plop! The rat leaves perfect rings on the surface of the water.

"It's gone under again," shouts Harpy.

Unknown to the lads, the rat has swum deep.

Over time, underwater, the clever rodents have hollowed out a fallen tree trunk, with a small hidey-hole above the water line. The rat has crawled into this hole and exhausted, is clinging to its safe haven within the log. Shivering in the dark, with only one watery entrance and exit, the rat is safe as long as it stays there and remains quiet.

Redwing arrives and starts to bang the log with his club. The vibration shakes the log but the rat has a firm grip on the wooden interior and knowing it's safe, sets about preening itself.

From across the river, Harpy shouts, "That's it, lads, it's gone to ground."

But a determined Redwing isn't giving up and ushers Buck back into the water. Buck did as he was told, but the scent is lost.

"Hey! Never mind that rat, my ferret's not come out yet," Velvet calls, fed-up with waiting.

Responding to their pal's cry, Ricky and Harpy go back to the original site.

Redwing stays by the log, sure the rat will reappear when he lights 'Britain's great little cigarette.'

After their exertions, the lads are cooling down. Their feet cold, Ricky and Harpy shiver in the cool morning. Velvet is still expectant that his ferret will emerge. Harpy is just about to shout, "There," but quickly realises it is only a sparrow darting in to pick up some insect from a fallen leaf.

Redwing finally gives up his vigil and moves up stream to a shallow section of river. Here he gingerly skips over some stones to cross over and join his mates sitting, watching and waiting for Velvet's ferret to re-surface.

Redwing's instincts tell him that something is wrong. He gets to his feet and goes to inspect the hole. Kneeling, he takes a long suck on his Woodbine and with his cheeks full of the blue vapour, he blows the toxic gas down the hole and then stuffs his boot across the mouth of the hole.

"That should flush it out," says Redwing.

"Hey! You'll choke my ferret," says Velvet.

"It needs choking. I think you've bought a right duffer," says Redwing.

"Give it a chance." says Velvet.

"A chance! It's been down there longer than the fucking devil," says Redwing.

Ricky complains, "I feel rap." "Like a crap," says Redwing.

"Noooo, just crap," says Ricky.

"If you want a crap; go behind the bushes." says Velvet.

"Crap off!" says Ricky.

"Here have a ciggy," says Redwing, 'it'll give you energy. It always works for me. Have ya not noticed, every time I light up something happens?"

"No chance, coltsfoot rock will do me thanks," Ricky replied.

"It'll rot your teeth, that rock," says Redwing.

"I can clean my teeth, but you can't clean your lungs," Ricky hit back.

"Hey! Shut up a minute," Redwing demands.

All instantly freeze, listening intently, trusting their scout's ear.

"There, can you hear it, it's coming from the tunnel?" says Redwing.

"Yes, it sounds like chopping." says Velvet.

"Must be in Madder Mill wood," says Redwing.

"Hey, come on, let's go through the tunnel and have a look, see what's going on," says Harpy.

"Might as well, there's fuck-all happening here," says Redwing.

Chapter 9

Part 3

Madder Mill Wood

Madder Mill wood is on the other side of the hill and can be accessed through a tunnel. About a mile long, the round tunnel is about eight feet in diameter and has a rough riverbed.

Leaving Velvet to mind his ferret, without hesitation and full of adventure, the boys set off to walk through the long dark tunnel and investigate what's going on in the wood.

Believing his feathers protect him, the wide-eyed Redwing leads the way. Holding on to his shoulder is Ricky and then Harpy, each trusting the one in front, following each other.

After only a few yards, the last of the guiding daylight is lost. The brook is shallow and the water moves slowly. Avoiding any slips on the slimy edges and ignoring the bats hanging asleep above their heads, they walk on into blackness. Concentrating hard and claiming he can see in the dark, Redwing presses on fearlessly.

The only sound is the cold air whispering in their ears and their wellies splashing through the water. Their hearts beat faster the deeper they go and the blinder they become. Any fears borne though are soon lost when Harpy starts to play his harmonica and Ricky sings 'Three Blind Mice,' the sounds reverberating off the Nori brick walls.

Meanwhile, beyond the tunnel, lost in their manual labour, no one at the exit can hear the boys singing. Except that is for the enterprising little 'Fingy' Worrell, who, sitting on a rock in the middle of the river, lifting his ear he's sure he can hear music coming from out the depth of the tunnel.

Ten minutes deep, Redwing rounds the bend and can see a spot of white light at the end of their watery trek. "Not long now," he shouts over the music. Each looks over the other's shoulder to also see the spot of light. In relief, Ricky sings louder and Harpy blows harder and in his croaky voice, Redwing sings bass. With their spirits rich, they kick through the water.

'Fingy' turns to see the trio emerge from the black hole. With a skip in their step, broad smiles and still singing, they arrive just in time to see their pal, big lad Max, and see his mass of black hair bounce and his belly judder when he strikes the final blow that fells an already dead twenty-foot Sycamore tree.

Using the only proper axe the ten or so Church Kirk boys have between them, Max has been working hard on the tree all morning.

Narrowly missing the rows of homemade trolleys, the dead tree crashes to earth, but standing too close, a flying splinter hits Ricky on the side of his head and draws blood.

"Sorry," says Max.

Feeling a lump growing, Ricky wipes his forefinger across the wound and sucks the sticky blood from his finger,

"Ah, it's all right, it's only a scratch, it'll be right," he says.

The dwarf lumberjacks have built trolleys to ferry the felled trees home. Constructed from any wooden planks found on the council's open tip, they have two large pram wheels at the back and two small scooter wheels at the front. Nails hammered through the wood and bent over, keep the axles fixed to the base.

Steering is by a rope nailed to the front wheel cross bar that swivels on a half-inch coach bolt. Coming in all shapes and sizes and various states of repair, it is doubtful if some will carry the weight of a tree! Costing nothing to build but time, to each Church Kirk lad it is his personal chariot. A few prams, hijacked from non-expectant mothers, accompany the trolleys. All the conveyors are waiting to ferry the felled timber the mile up and then down to the bonfire site on the spare ground beside the canal at the bottom of Donkey Back. Its name is known from times past as the track used by donkeys to ferry coal from the now disused mine to the canal barges.

The collection of anything that will burn on the bonfire in four days' time is in earnest. The area is alive with activity, with most lads busy working hard hacking away at the dead tree trunks. Two to a tree, there are competitions to see who will fell theirs first. Some bored with or taking a break from the chopping, play on a rope swinging from a tree. A few are climbing trees to retrieve conkers; others are picking them off the ground. Some, with conkers already threaded on string, are in full combat, but the ripe soft flesh easily disintegrates on the first hit so there will be no sixers on this day.

To bring down the trees, the gangs are using a fearsome collection of axes, machetes and butchers' cleavers. Some of the tools are sharp, but the majority are blunt and have jagged edges, despite vain attempts to sharpen them on any available stone surface. Fingy is taking the chance to earn a few pennies, trying his best to sharpen them on a hard stone in the middle of the river.

Proudly looking down at the fallen tree, Max proclaims, "this is ... gonna be biggest bonfire yet."

Seeing the bonfire boys are going to be busy all day, the ratters leave them to get on with it and set off back to check on Velvet. They re-enter the tunnel, but change the tune: "Ah Ah Ah, Hee Hee Hee; Little brown jug don't I love thee, Ah Ah Ah, Hee Hee Hee; Elephants nests in a rhubarb tree ..."

Returning, the trio greets a brooding Velvet, "You alright, pal?"

"No, I'm not; the ferret's still down the hole," he says.

Redwing is suspicious; only once has he known a ferret stay down so long and, on that occasion, he had to leave it and never saw it again.

White clouds are strolling across a calm blue sky, and because the sun has risen to its autumnal height, the day has warmed up, so the ratters settle down and are drying out.

Harpy stops sucking on his second Domino. "Well, we can't leave without the ferret; ya know the goodun, can we?" he says sarcastically.

Sitting on his left boot, a Woodbine between two brown fingers Redwing has his back against a Beech tree, his right leg bent to support his elbow on his knee.

His wellies hanging upside down on sticks to drain, and his socks draped over a branch to dry in the sun, sitting in front of the hole resting his white feet on dry leaves, Ricky is sucking on a stick of coltsfoot rock. Wringing out the bottom of his jeans, he wonders what is going on down there.

Copying Ricky, Harpy has also taken off his wellies and set them to drain, and his socks to dry. Sitting on a boulder above the river, his wrinkled feet dangling over the water, Harpy taps his harmonica on his knee, freeing it from any dirt or water, then, while each dog is either sitting or lying asleep beside its owner, he starts playing an old tune the brook had taught him.

Now that the drama of the hunt has died away and with the sweet and clear sound from Harpy's playing, an ambience of calm has embraced the copse. The music seems to have cast a spell upon the birds, who seem to be singing louder as they flutter about in their tireless search for food.

A cock pheasant and his wife are perched on a fence by a Sycamore tree. Redwing is tempted to have a shot at them, but his sharp eye measures the distance. "Too far," he thinks.

Anyway, Harpy has only two cartridges and is hoping to bag a rabbit or two, so he thinks it better to save them for an easier target. But it did not stop him from taking aim and setting his sights on them, nodding in confidence that he could have bagged both.

From their side of the river, the boys can hear a flock of starlings chattering and watch them assemble in their favourite roosting places in the trees. Some are already perched in the upper branches, but some are slow to settle and take their time, swooping to and fro, unfolding bizarre patterns in the sky. Black and white magpies arrive, their cackle drowning out the starlings' discussions. Redwing starts counting the magpies, reciting to himself, "One for sorrow, two for joy, three for a girl, four for a... four for a... Oh, bollocks; five, six, seven..."

Velvet has picked some blackberries from a nearby bramble and is nibbling at the sweet fruit, tasting the native soil in the dappled sunshine of this fine morning. The boys' eyes wander around the copse, they see and hear blackbirds, chaffinch, song thrush, woodpigeon, greenfinch, rook, crow, robins and wrens. A pair of busy red squirrels appear and disappear, but come back curious to what's going on in their copse.

Still nothing happening from underground, Redwing gets himself up and steps forward. He drops his cigarette stub and screws it out with his boot. Lying near the hole face down, he raises his hand and places a finger across his lips, asking the others to be quiet. The keen scout places his ear to the ground to listen. After a few seconds, his eyes roll, they brighten and a smile grows across his thin lips. "Scuffling, scuffling, I can hear scuffling," he whispers.

Meanwhile, deep underground, in the dead-end pitch-black cavern, two opalescent demon eyes hold her prey in a terrified trance. Closing in, the sleek assassin slows her advance. Her four limbs held taut, her back arched, the ghostly hunter springs, sinking into her needle teeth. Her hungry jaws crunch a skull, and a dry tongue sips the spilt brains, gnawing through tough fur to gorge on the heart and liver. Then, upon a clean straw nest, the sated ferret rolls on to her back, her little legs limp. Those dead pink eyes blink; she sleeps!

"About fucking time," says Harpy. "Yeh, we could have been well down the river by now," says Ricky.

"It'll be all right; at twelve and six, it's got to be a goodun," says Velvet.

Nevertheless, having missed out on the chase and their skittish comments, Velvet is becoming ever more agitated.

A half hour passes by.

"Hey Redwing, check out the hole. What the hell's going on down there? Why hasn't it come out?" asks Velvet. Comfortable in his squatting position, arms resting on bent knees, "I told you it were a duffer," says Redwing. But he rises, moves forward and throws himself to the ground.

With his ear to the hole, he listens. This time, his eyes don't brighten, they darken. Lowering his eyebrows, he frowns.

Watching Redwing's gloomy expressions, Velvet's eyes bulge, his face reddens with anger. Waving his arms, he shrieks,

"What?" and louder, "What, what?"

Concentrating harder and longer to check what he hears is correct, Redwing ignores Velvet's ranting, then issuing himself a sly grin, turns his black eyes up to the pop-eyed Velvet and places a nicotine-stained finger across his pursed lips.

"Sh-sh-sh-sh… yer good un is sleeping—it's slept in, has fallen asleep," he whispers.

Too angry to think of what to do next, Velvet circles, stomping the ground.

Wringing his hands so hard, the glass stone in his ring cuts into his palm. Bleeding and feeling cheated, he empties his pockets of stones, says, "Don't do anything till I come back," and sets off running up the path.

With nothing to do but wait for Velvet's return, the boys relax …

"There! There!" Harpy shouts.

Down at the riverbank, with Harpy carrying Redwing's club in hot pursuit, they see Bon Appetit paddling across the river and a rat swimming for the far bank. The others look on as both dog and boy reach the opposite bank. At the same time, the rat emerges from the water's edge. Distracted by a 'plop' to his left, Harpy spins round quickly only to see Redwing grinning, having mischievously thrown in a pebble. Harpy turns back and seeing the rat, instinctively he strikes with a club, missing the rat completely, the blow belting Bon on the head just before she closes her jaws on the scrambling rodent.

As the rat runs through the grass, Harpy stares in horror, numb and oblivious to the cold river overflowing his wellies.

Stifling to laugh out loud, wearing forced serious expressions, Ricky and Redwing call out,

"Au revoir, Bon Appetit," as the limp carcass floats over the weir.

"Well! That's fucked it." says Redwing.

"No point in looking for her, she'll be over the weir by now," says Ricky.

Harpy drops his head, his shoulders sag holding back the tears.

Hardened towards death, Redwing quickly moves the conversation on.

"Hey! Ricky, I see Frankie Talbot's out of nick," he says, as they make their way back to the original hole.

"Scrine!" Ricky corrected, "he were in Borstal; not nick, weren't he?"

"Well, he's out now anyway, I saw him the other day. He looks bloody rough," says Redwing.

"What were he in for anyway?"

"Flogging lead off church roof, I think," Harpy chirps in.

"Yeah," Ricky says, "Mr Cavannagh caught him."

"Church warden?" asked Redwing

"Aye," says Ricky, "he'd have got away with it if he hadn't fell off roof, and Mr Cavannagh had to call ambulance!" "He's a useless git, ind he?" says Redwing.

"He's a good mate of yours Ricky, isn't he?" asks Harpy, sarcastically.

"I don't think so," Ricky says, "I haven't forgotten about that time we found him in our bathroom."

"Thieving little bastard," says Redwing.

"He can't fight either, can he Ricky?" asked Harpy.

"He shouldn't have insulted Shirley, should he?" Ricky answers.

"Yeah, you put up a good scrap for a poncy piana player," says Redwing.

"Eh! Less of the poncy," says Ricky.

"Well, it's about time you snogged that girl of yours. Anyway, you'd better look out for him because he's out," says Redwing.

Twenty minutes have passed before Velvet returns.

He has brought with him a spade, and starts to dig, chuntering to himself, "there's no way I'm gonna leave a ferret that cost me half-a-fucking crown. I could have bought a new pair of wellies; or twenty Park Drive!"

Following the line of the hole, the lads agree to take turns to dig. While he waits his turn, musing over the ferret, Harpy recollects on the time he set out one morning with Shan, a bitch dog he borrowed from his neighbour, Andy Black.

Retelling the story, Harpy says: "I collected my ferret from the allotment in the morning to go and catch a rabbit for tea. We'd been out for a while before Shan marks this rabbit hole, over by Coppy Clough. I pulled my ferret from its bag and laid it to the hole. Ferret slowly moved down the burrow and I pulled Shan back to wait for the rabbit to bolt. After about five minutes, I hear rustling coming from the bushes nearby. First, a greyhound appears and then the face of Les Talbot!"

"Oh shit! I thought. Les shoves his way forward through bushes and says, 'Hey up Harpy, what's going on here then?' I had to tell him my ferret is in the hole and it were pushing a rabbit out. You know what the Talbots are like! Then he says, 'That rabbit's mine when it comes out.'"

"I looked up and thought bastard. But, him being cock of the school, I couldn't say anything. I did notice though; his jeans were held up with a piece of sugar string and his fly were held together with a pink safety pin.

"A squeal came from the rabbit hole. I turned and see the head of the rabbit looking out, judging which way to run, its frightened eyes looking side to side. Anyway, it makes it mind up quick, cos I guess the ferret were close behind. Rabbit runs to the left away from Shan and quick enough to avoid Les's grab as he moved forward.

"Next thing, at the same moment Les's safety pin gives way. The ferret appears looking for the rabbit, but all it sees is Les's fly spread wide and his lob pops out. Smelling cheese, the ferret takes a lunge at it. Les jumps back, cursing. Next thing I hear Harry Rhubarb,

"Rhubarb? Rhubarb?"

"Fuck off Harry!" Les shouts. Angry as fuck he were."

"Then, while Les's distracted, I grab my ferret, whistled for Shan, who'd caught the rabbit, and we scamper through bushes, leaving Les looking for his safety pin and still cursing."

"He'd have fucking hammered me, if he'd a caught me," Harpy admits,

"Hey! Come on, you two, stop yer yapping and have a dig," says a tiring Velvet, wiping his brow with his sleeve and kicking a large rock. "The hole goes under there."

Redwing moves forward, tightens up his shirt sleeves and flexes his biceps. Stretching his arms out wide, he holds his head up to the sky and howls to the wind before launching himself into the dig. His long hair swinging from side to side, some strands sticking to his sweating head, he pulls out the rock that's stopping progress with barehanded brute force. His phlegm-filled lungs are heaving under the effort; he snaps and removes any underlying tree roots. Stopping to catch his breath, with dirt-stained fingers, he parts the curtain of hair stuck to his wet face.

Redwing's pause gives Buck his chance. Keen as mustard, he forces his way between his master's legs and shoves his snout deep into the hole, sucking the scent of anything present through his nose. Then, breathing through the sides of his slavering mouth, he blows a snort into the hole, announcing to anything inside that he (Buck) is on his way.

Planting his back paws in the soil, Buck braces his hind legs and with expert balance, his two front paws moving in the reciprocating motion of an Olympic cyclist, he digs down. The speed and power of his paws throw the earth high, filling the air like a fountain and spraying all that stays too close. Even the other dogs turn their backs or scurry away from the force of the earthen shower. Moving his rear end from side to side to widen the hole and make room for his muscular shoulders, he distributes soil evenly over the ground, making sure not to miss anyone from their dose of dirt in the eye.

From time to time, Buck pulls his head out of the hole, blinking, his face and shoulders covered in the brown earth, his eyelashes caked in soil, panting and slavering. The

Lurcher looks around to check that everyone is still there. Redwing gets up to look, but Buck growls. Redwing throws his hands up and says, "All right, all right, carry on, carry on."

The beige dog pauses to brush his forepaw across his eyes to remove some soil, squinting at the thin worm crawling across his snout. Backing up to push accumulated earth to the rear to make space for more, he resets himself, shoves his snout down the hole and starts digging again.

The boys and dogs relax. Velvet takes a look at the site. There are stones, soil, clumps of clay, sods and roots scattered all about and the hole has now become a small cave. He thinks to himself, "this must be biggest dig, ever."

His head buried deep; Buck blows a loud snort. Digging faster, he starts to whinny, a sure sign to Redwing that he is getting close to the quarry.

"Call him off!" shouts Velvet.

"Come on Buck. Out! Out!" Redwing calls.

"Call him off! I don't want him to kill the ferret," shouts an agitated Velvet.

But Buck, knowing he is close, turns his head, gives Redwing the evil eye and growls, his way of saying 'no chance,' and carries on digging. Annoyed that he has to get up, Redwing screws his cigarette into his ear hole to free both hands and using the lead twice wrapped around Buck's shoulders, he applies all his strength to pull the protesting earth-covered Lurcher away from the hole.

Harpy volunteers for the last leg. By this time, the hole has moved to the left, to the right, forward, down, and back up again. The digging has excavated a large pile of earth and rubble. At first barely visible in the undergrowth, the tiny rat hole is now a large scar on the riverbank. Finally, after two hours of hard work, the bottom of the hole is there and they can see straw (the rat's nest) and the white tip of the ferret's tail.

"Right, I'll take charge," claims Velvet.

"Charge! A charge o' fuckin dynamite," quips Redwing, "would have been quicker than digging.

"Yeah," agrees Velvet, then looking down at the few white hairs, "at least I've found a name for it eh. Here she is; Rip van Winkle."

"Rip van Winkle?" Ricky says. "More like Beethoven! It must be fucking deaf. Ya, that's what's wrong with it, it's fucking deaf. Not waking up to all noise we've been making. You've paid twelve and six for a fucking deaf ferret."

Even more angry, Velvet removes the last of the earth that covers his twelve shillings and six pence, lying there motionless and oblivious to the attention that has been paid to it for the last couple of hours.

Old Gilbert Rishton once observed that the combined eruptions of Mounts Etna and Vesuvius have nothing on Velvet when he loses his temper, but, because of the infrequency, what comes next shakes the others to the very soles of their Wellington boots.

A lone black cloud moves in front of the sun, robbing the copse of all colour. In the ominous grey light, dark blood throbbing in the temple, Velvet's anger gained the better of his reason, and to everyone's wide-eyed astonishment, he threw the sleeping albino high into the air, grabbed Harpy's gun, cocked both barrels, aimed, and pulled the first trigger closely followed by the second.

The volley bellowed in the copse and reverberated throughout the Dunkenhalgh Park valley. For a long moment, there was chaos as all wild life either flew or bolted for cover.

Beauty, Buck and Tan accustomed to the blast of a gun, follow their masters' gaze and look skyward. The plump airborne ferret's shattered body decorated the whole group and the surrounding trees with blood and white fur.

After the last echo of the devastating rounds has faded, a stunned silence visits the grey valley; everything is still pensive, and sad. Then the bells of St.

James's begin to peal sonorously in the distance, snapping the boys out of their silence and breaking the morbid mood.

"You cruel fucking bastard," says Redwing.

"Serves it right, the dozy bastard," says Velvet.

Harpy is too stunned to comment; as far as he's concerned, his last two cartridges are wasted.

"Sorry about that, Harpy," says Velvet.

"Bollocks!" says Harpy.

The black cloud passes on by. Bird song replaces the bells that are fading away in the distance. Velvet, Harpy and Ricky bury what they could find of the scattered creature.

Redwing, using his Bowie knife, some river driftwood and string he's unthreaded from a discarded fertiliser bag, cobbles together a cross and, trusting Velvet's translation, carves into the damp grey wood the inscription, 'Ago non obdormio post epulae." (Don't fall asleep after dinner.)

The copse is once again full of colour. With heads bowed and hands clasped in front, the four ratters stand in a circle around the tiny grave with its pathetic crooked cross. Back in control of his senses, using his velvet tongue in his best Latin parlance, Velvet utters a little prayer he's quickly composed for the deceased and the twelve shillings and sixpence he has, just a short time ago, blown away.

> Sit acceptio cororis tui,
> Terra incipit consumer;
> Hic sepultus est hodie
> ad meridiem Calcare
> flores crescere in June
> Intus huic opaco.

> Andy Nigrum dixit velis esse victor

Et non perdet viam
vestram Vel
perperam; solet
praeda cotidie Intus
reat, ut OK!
'sed post cenam non doriunt.'

Let the receiving of thy corpse
The earth begins to consume
Buried here today at noon,
Spur flowers to grow in June
Within this shady copse.
Andy Black says you'd be a winner
And never lose your way
Or stray; flush your prey every day
Eat inside, that's OK!
'But don't fall asleep after dinner.'

The others, eyes down, are unaware of the content of
the prayer, but trusting their pal to say something profound,
all mutter a forlorn "amen." Harpy, with a tear in his eye,
plays The Last Post. Then Redwing, using a rattle he's made
with acorns and a tin can he found in the river, dances around
the grave and to assist the ferret's spirit on its journey along
the milky path, he chants …

ee yah yah wah nah aylay chee mah kah chay uhn nah
ghee aylay chee mah kah chay uhn nah
he he ya pe lo he he yo
he he ya pe lo he he yo.

Go now to the land of Souls
to the Land of Souls
this is what we say
this is what we say.

Feeling quite sad at the outcome of their day rather than excited by a successful hunting trip, the lads prepare to leave the trampled excavation. "Hang on!" Ricky shouts.

"What for?" asks Velvet.

"There's something here; it's silver. Have we left a fag packet behind?" Ricky asks.

Lifting the rat's nest out of the way, he uses his thumb and forefinger to grip the offending article, but he can't lift it, it is held too firm in the ground.

"Hey Redwing, lend me your knife?" asks Ricky. Redwing takes the bowie knife from its scabbard and throws it into the ground near Ricky.

"Thanks," says Ricky, pulling the blade free.

Then, carefully he scrapes away the earth and frees what, from memory, he now recognises.

"Hey! Velvet, you should have called your ferret, Roger!"

He holds the find high and says,

"What about that, then, eh? Now this is a good un!"

"What the hell is it?" asks Velvet.

"I thought it was silver foil at first, but look."

He raises the object.

The others looked bemused.

"It's silver. Look, it's a silver chalice! I'll bet Roger de Rishton buried it here." Says Ricky.

"Roger?" asks Velvet. "Roger, who and why should I call my ferret, Roger?"

Redwing asks, "A chalice; what's one of them?"

"It looks like a fucking cup to me." Harpy says.

Taking the first question first, Ricky replies, "Roger... Roger de Rishton."

"Who is he?" demands Redwing.

Cleaning the chalice on his sleeve, "Roger de Rishton lived here in 1537 or something like that. Anyway, it was a long time ago, and..."

Tucking the Chalice into his inside jacket pocket, Ricky begins to tell his granddad's tale as they trudge their way back into civilisation.

When, half way up the rutted path, a very loud 'Yap Yap Yap' from behind interrupts Ricky's tale.

Turning to look, Redwing points with his chin and says, "Hey! Look there."

Everyone turns to see Bon Appetit racing up the hill, her little tail wagging allegro and yapping as if to say, "Hey, wait for me."

"Well, Harpy, it looks like you've got a real survivor there," says Velvet.

Ears flapping, red tongue lapping the air, Bon rushes up and leaps into Harpy's arms, licking his shocked face with joy.

"I think you've been forgiven," says Redwing.

Chapter 10

November 1957, Part 4

The Thief.

Unknown to anyone, in the early hours of the same morning, a small hand dropped the latch on Muriel's back door; as usual, she'd left the door unlocked! With the aid of a tiny torch, the intruder steered his way through the kitchen, the living room and into the shop at the front of her corner terraced house. The intruder stood on a stool and pressed an ivory key on the cash register. Together, a cream-coloured flag with blue 2/6d pops up in the glass window of the register and its bell rang, the cash drawer flew open and banged the thief on his head. Startled, he slipped off the stool and fell.

Blood trickling down his temple, he got up and froze—listening for any movement from Muriel. But he needn't have worried. Ten years a widow, the elderly Muriel, full of Guinness, was sound asleep.

Waiting until he was sure there was no movement from upstairs, he removed all the loose change and the one red ten-shilling note.

Filling his pockets with sweets, he made his way to the back of the house. Nearing the back door, he touched the wound, feeling it warm and wet. In the shop, fear of being caught had numbed the pain, but with the feeling of freedom being near, his fear had subsided and his head started to throb. With tears filling his eyes, he melts into the night.

After breakfast, with her black cat 'Ginny' tucked securely under her arm, Muriel shuffled her way into the shop and to compensate for the poor daylight filtering through the stained-glass lights, she pulled the chain to lower and light the oil lamp. This done, she walked to the front door, removed the top and bottom bolts and opened the shop for the day's business.

Almost before she turned to walk back behind the counter, the shop bell rang and waiting on the doorstep was her first customer, her old friend Gilbert. Resting his leg on the scrubbed high step he greeting her with a "Morning Muriel."

Holding the door open to let him in, "Morning Gil," says Muriel.

Her skirts brushing the floor, she sailed around the counter like a galleon in full flow.

Gilbert walked along the path of bare flagstones exposed through the dark green gloss floor paint to the counter.

Without asking and with an easy smile, Muriel placed a packet of St. Bruno on the counter. Taking Gil's money, she moved to the cash register for change.

"Oh my god, my till's empty!" She cried and fell back against the distempered green wall, the jars of sweets juggling on the shelves above.

"Are you sure?" says Gilbert, leaning over the counter to look into the drawer. "Did you not take the money out last night?"

"No. I never do, unless there are a few notes to put away, but there was only one ten-shilling note and some change," she says.

Checking his pockets for two-penny pieces, Gilbert says, "I'll go down to the telephone box and call Handy," leaving Muriel wondering who and why.

The village policeman, nicknamed 'Handy Pandy' because of the size of his hands, luckily turned the corner of the school before Gil made it to the phone box.

"Look!" Muriel says to Handy, "there's blood on the floor."

Handy looked down and saw a trail of dried blood on the white squares of the chequered lino on her kitchen floor.

Noticing the blood was thickest beneath the cash register, he scraped a few hairs and blood into the brown envelope.

****

At home, stuffing a raspberry jam butty down his throat, Ricky wonders what Roger de Rishton would have eaten in mischievous haste when he buried the Chalice and whether he would have washed it down with a cup of hot tea when a knock on the door interrupts his pondering.

"Hey, come on! We need you. There's a game on," Velvet urged.

"All right, all right, just give me a minute," says Ricky.

After feeding the dogs with Chappie, he removes his wellies, gingerly pulls his socks off, and peels off the polo-mint dressing covering the verruca on his left heel. With a new plaster on the threepenny bit growth, remembering he has to go to the doctors on Tuesday for him to scrape away the dead skin, he pulls on some clean socks and black canvas pumps, being careful to make sure the hole cut into the rubber sole on his left pump is on top of the verruca.

Before passing through the kitchen door, he casts his eyes around the kitchen, looking for something more to eat. He sees three trays cooling on the window sill, all cut into squares: one of treacle toffee, another gingerbread cake and the third tray loaded with rosy toffee apples placed in rows with their lolly sticks standing erect. Mrs. Rishton had cooked all of these early this morning in preparation for bonfire night.

Looking too good to resist, he peels off two semi-solid pieces of treacle toffee, stuffs one into his mouth and while holding the other in his left hand, carefully eases out a couple of slices of the gingerbread cake and puts them with care into the side pocket of his corduroy jacket. With tacky fingers, he tightly grips the lolly stick of one toffee apple and rocks it to and fro until it comes loose. Then, with a toffee apple in one hand, a square of treacle in the other and a mouthful of toffee glueing his teeth together, he runs from the house to join in the game.

But he is held up by a spud gun, loaded with a King Edward potato.

Wiping his dripping nose with his jacket sleeve and holding his pants to save them from falling, "Eh, got a penny, Fingy? Eh, got a penny?" quizzes Fingy, 'now you know why he's called Fingy.'

"Oh! All right, pal," says Ricky. "Sorry, I've got nothing on me, but here, take some of my mum's gingerbread," and bending down, he lets Fingy take a slice of cake from his pocket.

Fingy's eyes light up and he stuffs the whole piece into his mouth. "Cheers Fingy," he splutters and runs off to find another punter.

Ricky sets off, running onto the tarmac field of dreams.

"Richard, have you a minute?" asks Handy.

Handy Pandy never referred to the boys by their nick-names.

Ricky's heart beats faster and a lump fills his throat.

Swallowing hard, "yes," says Ricky.

"That scratch on your face, where did you get it?" Handy asks.

Ricky moved his hand up to the scratch. "I got it down the Dunk this morning, we were out ratting," he answers nervously.

"We?" queried Handy.

"Me, Velvet, Harpy and Redwing," says Ricky.

"Are you sure, were you not out earlier this morning?" asks Handy, with extra emphasis on earlier.

Not yet having heard about the robbery, Ricky looked up at Handy questioningly. "No, well, not really early; we set off about seven," he says.

Taking a long look at the colour of Ricky's brown hair, Handy says, "OK, you can go on; have a good game." Relieved he had been released, Ricky runs to join in the game, wondering what that was all about.

****

Ricky joins the game of street football. Played on the tarmac road between the Thorn Inn and St. James' Churchyard gates. The wrought-iron gates at the entrance to the churchyard had been removed for the war effort in 1939 and have never been replaced, but the statuesque sandstone pillars remain and provide two natural goalposts. The inn's green wooden double yard gates act as the opposite goal.

A stench from the tallow works has replaced this morning's smell from the chemical works and the pungent aroma drifts across the playground on a light breeze.

In this acrid atmosphere, Ricky joins in with the growing group of boys and is waiting to see whose side he will be on.

Captain Velvet shouts, "All right, settle down. Me first. In goal, I'll take Redwing."

Captain Harpy, "In goal, Seddy." "Ricky," says Velvet.

"Froggy," chooses Harpy.

And so it goes, until the teams are decided.

Velvet wins the toss, throws the ball overhead to start the game and shouts, 'Kick off'!

There are no designated forwards, fullbacks, or midfielders; they are all utility players. With everyone chasing the ball in earnest, they move across the tarmac like a flock of starlings looking for somewhere to settle. As is usual, whoever wins the toss wins the game and after only five minutes of play, the score is 3-1 to Velvet's team.

Not wearing a team kit means mistakes are often made. Some forget whose side they are on and pass the ball to the opposition or even score their own goals, which always introduces some new words to the English language.

On Harpy's side, Froggy tackles Velvet, wins the ball and heads for goal. But drawing back his foot to shoot, his black canvas pump catches the lip of a manhole cover and rips his sole off from toe to midfoot, hanging like a torn pocket. Unable to run without tripping over, Froggy flaps around in front of the opposition's goal, being a goal liner.

The score is now 4-2 to Velvet's team.

In front of the goal, "here, here," Ricky shouts madly.

The ball up in the air, Velvet, Redwing, Harpy and Froggy all challenge for it, but collide in a heap when it comes back to ground.

"Here," Ricky screams again, "here."

Overexcited, Seddy ignores Ricky and shoots for the goal.

In goal, Tall Tony catches the shot in his long arms and quickly throws the ball to his pal, Dave, who races to the opposition goal. "Go on, Dave, shoot!" shouts Tall Tony. Ricky gives chase and tackles him before he can fire a shot. The ball ricochets to Harpy, who slices the ball over the inn gates.

"You pillock," says Ricky. Harpy's head drops in disappointment.

"You'd better get over and get it," says Redwing.

Harpy climbs over the wall and finds the ball wedged under the exhaust of Bill's Ford Popular. He looks around the yard for something long enough to reach the ball and free it. The only thing is the pole holding up the washing line, which is frustrating to Harpy because it's full of wet clothes, and if he takes it down, the clean washing will fall on top of the car.

"Come on, Harpy! What are you doing?" Velvet shouts. Under pressure, Harpy decides to go for it. Grasping the square pole with both hands, he gently eases down the clothes and rests them on the car roof.

Meanwhile, standing around waiting for the ball to come back into play, the boys start talking between themselves.

"Did you hear about Muriel being robbed?" asks Velvet.

"Robbed, what was all that about?" says Ricky.

"Early this morning, somebody broke into her shop and took some money," says Velvet.

Ricky stays silent and Velvet thought it curious for his mate not to enquire further. He knew that he usually wants to know everything that goes on. Velvet took a hard look at his pal.

Fearing being spotted from the side window; Harpy drops to the ground and works the pole under the car to nudge the ball free. The ball rolls down the yard, so he jumps up quickly. Being careful in replacing the pole and washing to its previous height, he gathers the ball, sighs in relief and throws it back into the game.

Most players have taken their jackets or jumpers off and have piled them up behind the green cast iron lamp post. Back in play, like a tide ebbing and flowing, they are all chasing the ball from one set of goals to the other. The wind has turned and a gentle breeze from Dunkenhalgh Park sweeps in a sweeter smell from the fields, refreshing the arena.

"Incoming," Harpy shouts. Curious to know what is coming, following his gaze, everyone stops to look down the lane. Seeing nothing, they all turn to Harpy and ask, "What?"

"Listen," Harpy urges.

A muffled boom from somewhere within the labyrinth of terraced houses can be heard and is getting louder. Then black smoke fills the street at the bottom of the Lane.

The source is soon visible and they all recognise Jeff McVeigh on his pea green Excelsior 125cc two-stroke motorcycle, its fractured exhaust coughing out rings of black smoke. Inside his goggles, Jeff's eyes bulge in concentration, with his black hair pinned smooth to his red scalp and his 'Stanley' shirt billowing and baggy blue jeans flapping. In his sockless black canvas pumps, a callused big toe, worn raw, clicks through the gears. Leaning over the petrol tank to streamline his profile, he races towards the crowd, then slows and rises up from his seat. Wearing a huge grin, he places one foot on the saddle and, using his other foot to steer the bike, turns sideways to view his audience and rides through them, his arms raised. His audience part and cheer encouragement.

Turning at the church, he makes several passes in different positions, entertaining everyone. That is everyone except Bill, who comes out of the inn to complain about the noise blowing from the bike's exhaust. Forced to abandon his acrobatic display, an act worthy of any circus show, Jeff switches the ignition off, props his bike against Mastabar's wall and with his adoring fans patting him on the back, he joins the game.

The afternoon moves on, and the teams and the folks watching have grown. There are now about 20–25 lads and lasses, creating an exciting, energetic atmosphere in this small, isolated enclave.

A fair, organised by the Mother's Union, the Men's Society and the United Class, which has both men and women members, is being held on the spare ground behind the church. The bell ringers have remained from their morning session to make their contribution to raising money for the upkeep of the church, and the melodious sound of the bells mixing with the loud voices of the players and spectators resonated around the arena.

The church caretaker, Mr. Cavannagh, has mowed the grass short and planted colourful blooms of peony and pansy along the edges of the pathways. Behind the church there are various stalls and sideshows, including bring and buy stalls selling sweets, chocolates, handkerchiefs and tinned goods.

There's a breaking-the-crockery stall, a coconut shy and a darts alley, all run by members of church organisations.

Howard & Bullough Cotton Mill Youth Club, invited in from nearby Accrington, have arranged a display of physical training.

As the football teams have grown, so has the score, chalked on a flat stone near the left pillar.

In red, it reads, Harpy 10. In yellow, Velvet 15.

Handy Pandy, though, is not interested in the score. All he can think of is the crime committed on his patch. Still unsure who the culprit is, he moves amongst the players and spectators, asking questions.

From his front door, Edgar shouts, "Richard, Richard!"

Ricky stops and turns to face his dad. "I've got a job this afternoon; I'll be digging a grave in the cemetery, so can you go down to the pen and get a chicken for tonight's tea?" Oh! And a rabbit; I'll bake a pie for tomorrow's dinner."

Energised at the thought of rabbit pie and dumplings, obediently but with a sense of unease about the task at hand, Ricky gives his dad the thumbs up and leaves the game. With the toffee apple long gone, he stuffs the last piece of treacle toffee into his mouth, sucks his fingers clean and wipes them dry on his jeans. He climbs the green cast-iron lamp post to retrieve his jacket he had left hanging over the ladder bar, then grabs his push bike, which he had assembled from salvaged parts found on the council tip. The only new fixtures are the white-walled tyres and the two air horns strapped together and mounted on the handle bars. One horn is tuned to 'di' the other to 'da' so he can play 'di–di–di–da," 'di–di–di–da'. The frame is brush painted in British Racing Green and has cow-horn handle bars with white push-on rubber grips attached. It has just one fixed gear and only one brake that grabs the chrome rim of the 26-inch back wheel. There are no mudguards. Winning bets as to whether he could climb up the side of his stone-built end-terrace house, on to and over the roof, touch the chimney and climb back down provided him with money for the tyres and the horns.

Ricky cocks his leg over the crossbar and pushes off. His legs are already pumped up from playing football, and seeing Shirley at the game lifts his spirits. He rides hard along St. James's Road, mindful of the promise that today will be the day he realises his dream to kiss her. He rides over the hump on the bridge and down the steep dirt path that leads to the allotment holdings. Passing the farm, he looks in to see Mr. Thomson cleaning up. Arriving at the allotment whistling, he props his bike up against the fence, places his jacket across the handlebars and unfastens the lock holding the pen gate shut.

On the allotment, Edgar keeps chickens, ducks and rabbits, all reared for the table. As well as the nourishing meat, the chickens provide eggs, which Ricky has to collect every morning before school. Sometimes these early morning runs make him late for school, but the bike has made it easier and quicker for him to get there and back. As well as livestock, there is also a small plot for growing vegetables—carrots, cabbage, lettuce and rows of sweet peas—some for their flowers, but some are left to seed or eaten in soups.

The rabbits are a crossbreed of New Zealand White and Flemish Giants, which produce a large rabbit with tender meat. Also on the pen are twelve chickens, all served by one rooster called Strauss, and six white ducks. The selection of which chicken to kill is down to the first one he can catch. After ten minutes of chasing around the pen, he catches one and out of sight from the others, he twists its neck and pulls. Plucking it while it is still warm. Bred for the table only, he's learned not to treat them as pets and not to have any names or favourites. However, having fed them every day since they were born and even talked to them when he needed someone to talk to, killing one is always hard. But dad says he had to bring one back and you do not argue with your dad. You had to get on with it.

Now for the rabbit. From previous 'stressful' experiences, he knows he shouldn't linger about which one.

A large buck had bitten him on a couple of occasions, but when he went in to change his water so quickly, he made the choice.

Approaching the hutch, the buck knows 'they both know' they are to play a part in a terrible act that neither wants to play in, but both are helpless in their parts. Hiding at the back of the hutch, his hind legs thumping the bottom of the cage, the feisty rabbit looks at him with accusing eyes. Ricky grabs it by the scruff of the neck and clumsily pulls it out of the hutch. Struggling to get a hold of its kicking back legs, he finally succeeds. His scrawny arms hold the rabbit upside down and tired from its effort to break free; the rabbit relaxes.

Taking advantage of the lull, Ricky strikes the back of its scull with the side of his hand in a chopping action, trying to break its neck, but misses. He strikes again, misses, and strikes again and again—painful blows for Ricky, but deadly for the rabbit; she hangs loose. Before beginning the skinning, he sits on an upturned log to rest for a few moments and becomes aware of cold silver eyes staring at him from each hutch and his face reddens. Gathering himself, he lays the limp carcass across an oak tree stump in the middle of the pen, pulls the butchers knife held in the hard wood and pierces the rabbit's stomach. The stench from the innards sends signals to his stomach to evacuate the raspberry jam butties, the apple, and the treacle toffee mixture. The only consolation is that they taste just as good coming up as they do going down.

He needs to keep the food down to give him energy to continue in the game, so he turns his head and nose away from the stench and with his hands on his hips, he takes long, deep gulps of fresh air to suppress the want to vomit. Settling, he continues to skin and gulp until the job is done.

His right hand is numb, an early sign of a bruise, but with the rabbit killed, gutted and skinned, he ties its bare legs with sugar string and having slung it around his neck with the naked chicken, he sets off to leave the allotment. At the gate, he stops and his bottom jaw falls. "My bike, it's gone!" He then realises that the chalice is in the inside pocket of his hunting jacket. Whoever has taken his bike has tossed his jacket into a ditch. He picks it up and checks the pockets; they're empty! The Chalice it's also gone!

"Oh shit!" he cries. "I must have forgotten about the chalice in the rush to get my dinner down and then Velvet banging on the door; I hadn't taken it out."

"Oh, fuck! It's been nicked; underground for fifteen hundred years, four hours of freedom and it's been nicked *again*," he cries out loud. Scanning the paths leading away from the allotments to see if he can spot the culprit, he sees nothing and no-one. He checks his pockets again. "Bastard, fuck me, they've even pinched my gingerbread." Silent and astounded, he puzzles over why the bastard thief has not taken his jacket.

Lamenting his lost property, he pulls himself together and locks the pen gate. Then, dragging his feet, all the way home he hopes no one tells his granddad that he found the Chalice, only to lose it again. He knows his granddad will be saddened.

Back home, in the kitchen, he gives the fresh meat to his dad, who, seeing him sulking, asks, "You look like you've seen your ass and don't like the colour of it; what's up?" Ricky explains about his bike and the Chalice.

"Don't worry, son, we'll find them," says Edgar, and then more philosophically, "all things return."

Feeling a little better after his dad's assurance, he rejoins the game. Immediately, he notices a few faces are missing.

"Where have they all gone?" he asks.

"Tree-climbing contest," says Harpy, pointing towards the churchyard. With the game stopped, Ricky goes into the churchyard to watch.

Chapter 11

November 1957, Part 5

Tree Climbing Contest.

In the grounds at the front of St. James', there are fourteen Sycamore and two Beech trees, eight lining the pathway leading to the nave door and eight around the perimeter wall.

To ensure each competitor reaches the top, using chalk 'nicked' from school, a white mark is made near the top branch of each tree for the climbers to touch. Speed tree climbing contests can be a five, ten or even twenty-tree challenge, but with the football game on, the winner of today's contest will be the one who climbs five trees in the shortest time. Speed tree climbing takes a cool head, strength, agility and no fear, but all too often, it is proven that those who try too hard fail.

Among the challengers is the bespectacled Seddy, which surprises Velvet. Seddy suffers from epilepsy and sometimes has sudden convulsions, which render him helpless. Every time he sees him, Velvet recalls the lucky escape the youngster had when stealing fruit from the Dunkenhalgh orchard. When the chef came out, firing his shotgun in the air to scare them off, having to run for their lives, Seddy went into shock, fear rendering him speechless and motionless. Luckily, he froze behind a tree and the chef could not see him. Eventually he regained the use of his legs and catching up with the rest, he told Velvet how his hands and feet felt enormous and all over the place.

Speaking to Velvet, Ricky learns that a lad called Spuds, who has travelled from Accrington, has challenged Redwing, who, despite his bronchial handicap, is the champion in all categories. The other contestants are Froggy,

Tall Tony and, with a wide plaster across his nose, Batman, making six climbers in all.

Acting as referee, Velvet takes control and announces them in order according to their previous best time, starting with the slowest first.

This being Seddy's first attempt, Velvet announces, "Seddy, time unknown."

"Come on, Seddy," the gang encourages him.

"Come on, Seddy; get up there."

"You can do it, mate; go on."

Determined to overcome his fear of heights, Seddy sets off fast, reaching the top of the first tree surprisingly quickly. His supporters cheer until, flushed with success, on the second tree, he looks down. Immediately, his head starts to spin and his nervous system goes into remission. He hugs the tree; his glasses hang loose on one ear and he is too afraid to straighten them should he fall.

They leave him stuck to his tree like a Koala and as this tree is going to be occupied for some time, they have to use another first tree.

"Next, Batman, time six minutes and thirty-four seconds."

Using his primate-like frame to good effect, Batman easily scales trees one and two. He progresses well until the third, where he loses his grip and falls to the ground, luckily missing any branches on the way down.

"Next, Froggy, time five minutes and forty seconds."

Froggy concerns Redwing because, when he gets it right, he can climb with the best, even himself. "Come on, Froggy," his supporter's call. Redwing and Ricky watch from the pathway. Having strapped the sole of his damaged pump to the upper with masking tape, Froggy is about to touch the top of the fourth tree in good time until the tape on the pump that's bearing his weight snaps; he had only wrapped the paper tape around once. His foot turned on the loose sole and he slipped down the branch. Straddling an upper branch, the narrow limb breaks under his weight and he starts to descend. He breaks three branches on his way down before his momentum is brought to a sudden, painful stop on a thicker lower branch. His bid for glory ends with a badly bruised crotch. Stunned and in silent agony, he stares into space for a moment before sliding sideways off the branch, hitting the ground with a groan. Redwing unfolds Froggy and Tall Tony moves into position, eager to get started.

As Doris, the Thorn landlady, escorts Froggy away, Velvet pronounces, "Next climber is Tall 'the Ted' Tony, time five minutes and thirty-five seconds."

Feeling good in his brown 'ted suit', blue beetle crusher shoes, green fluorescent socks and black string tie, the six-foot-two Tony's long arms and legs haul him up the first tree quickly. Stretching to touch the first white mark, his crusher jams in the fork of the branch. Desperate to reach the mark, he tries to pull his crusher free but loses his grip and falls backwards. He is hanging upside-down; blood is filling his head and his face is turning purple. His stomach muscles are too weak to pull him up, so he starts shouting.

"Help! Help! Get me down, get me down."

"Teddy boys?" says Velvet, raising his eyebrow.

Redwing shoves Tony upwards and supports his weight, while Spuds unties his laces. Tony pulls his foot out of the shoe and lowers his long body down to the ground. His chance for 'Ted fame' is gone and his image is marred. He hobbles away with a sprained ankle, complaining about the scuffmarks on his shoes.

Waiting for the second finger to come round to twelve on his pocket watch, "Come on, Spuds, you're next," says Velvet.

"Spuds time, five minutes and twenty-two seconds."

His time being close to the record time, a 'whoo' ripples through the knowledgeable spectators.

Assisting Tony has warmed Spuds up. He sets a rapid pace and he is looking good enough to beat the existing record of five minutes and fifteen seconds for all five trees.

Eager to get going, Redwing doesn't wait to be introduced; with his hair tied back, he is ready at the bottom of the first tree. Giving Velvet just enough time to re-set his watch, the confident scout stuffs his burning Woodbine into his ear. Naturally athletic, Redwing's prowess carries him up and down trees one, two and three. Spuds comes down the fifth tree in a new record time of five minutes and six seconds. Keeping a close eye on Redwing's progress, those in the crowd with watches are getting nervous about losing their side bets. Redwing scampers up the fifth with sinuous grace, but, too eager, he slips, reaching for the final mark. Nevertheless, he recovers to place his feet at the bottom of the fifth in four minutes, fifty-two seconds. This ended Spuds' short reign, thus retaining and setting a new British, European, Commonwealth, and World record for the five-tree challenge. Celebrating his victory, Redwing dances to the tree God, chanting, "Five, ten, fifteen, twenty, it's all the same to me."

Chapter 12

November 1957, Part 6

The Fight.

Standing beside the Thorn Inn at the top of Kershaw Street, watching the lads, is a red-haired teenage girl. Her last name is Gordon. Everyone calls her Flash. She turns to her friend Shirley and asks, "Hey, isn't that your cousin coming up Donkey Back?"

Word soon spread of the outsider's approach. Everyone stops what he or she is doing to look towards the dirt track that runs parallel with St. James' churchyard wall and leads down to the Leeds and Liverpool canal.

When she sees who it is, Shirley's first thought is one of dread. She knows he is a fomenter of trouble that follows him wherever he goes. Her cousin is Mick Talbot; yes, a Talbot!

He stands at the centre of the back with the menace of a medieval executioner. His two cohorts, Scream and Scrine, acknowledging their lower status, keep a measured distance behind him.

"Hey!" Mick shouts. Then, certain he has everyone's attention, he reaches inside his denim bomber jacket and, like a conquering Roman tribune, triumphantly holds high the silver chalice.

Jaws open wide, Ricky stares at the chalice.

Velvet, Harpy and Redwing appear by Ricky's side, ready with their support. From behind Mick came two familiar notes and then Scrine came riding Ricky's stolen pushbike.

As if to taunt Ricky, Scrine, thin and pale after his Borstal internment, casts thievish glances, yet totally ignorant of the significance of the two notes, he blows the double-note horn, '*di-daa, di-daa*'.

His blood rising, Ricky wants to snatch the chalice, but knowing Mick will be too much of a handful for him, he makes a move to tackle Scrine and get his bike back.

Stepping forward, he feels a firm hand on his shoulder. He turns and looks up to see the smiling face of his cousin, Billy Rishton.

"I'll take care of this," says Billy.

Mick passes the Chalice to his second, known to all as Scream because of his resemblance to the character in the Edvard Munch painting.

"Come on, Rishton," says Mick, both hands gesturing before starting to thump his right fist into his left palm.

Welcoming the challenge of a Talbot entering the Rishton stronghold, his smile turning to a scowl, Billy shouts back, "You punk Talbot."

Ricky goes in search of Shirley. This encounter shows that the Rishton/Talbot feud of ancient times is still strong, and he wants to protect her and show her that he does not care if she is a Talbot.

Finding her was easy, for whenever there is peril, they somehow attract each other. Aggravated by the loss of his bike and seeing it in the possession of his enemy, the presence of Shirley calms and assures him.

They come close together and without speaking, their hands clasp. The touch of her female hand moves him. He shivers and again, as on so many occasions, he wants to kiss her. Squeezing her hand, he makes a promise to himself.

'Today, I will, I will'.

They melt into the crowd, becoming just two more spectators of the spectacle about to unfold before them.

Billy feels a wet touch on his palm, then a soft warmth on his fingers. He didn't look down to see who or what. He knows it is the wet nose and warm tongue of his best friend and Praetorian Guard, Sean, the handsome and aristocratic deerhound.

A fearsome warrior in his thick dark blue and grey coat, ragged and crisp to the touch, he covers the ground with ease and great dignity. His hazel eyes give a sweet, soft expression but a keen, alert look when aroused. A perfect specimen of his breed, he is brave, loyal and patient. Billy has fitted a tiny bell to his thick collar to warn people of his approaching bulk and with the bell jingling a happy tune, Sean sits by Billy's right hand.

Many others have joined those who had been playing football, forming a thirty-person circle around the two fighters and are whispering things like...

"Hey, there's a fight on."

"Who?"

"One's Billy."

"And that's Mick."

"Mick who?"

"He's one of them, Talbots."

"Didn't he get done for shooting a swan?"

"No, that's his brother, Les. Mick got done for flogging lead off the church roof."

"Who do you think'll win?"

"Billy, of course; whose side are you on?"

The boys, who are too small to play in the football game, playing marbles and the girls playing hopscotch or holding little doorway shops, selling toys and books, or outgrown discarded clothes, stop their activities and enterprises to mingle with the crowd. Some peer through their legs or, to gain an even better view, sit on their elder brothers' shoulders. Local cats interrupt their wanderings to sit on wall tops and window ledges. Pigeons, from chimney tops, and Rooks next to their untidy nests high in the churchyard trees, are watching. Everyone and everything, except the adults, it seems, have arrived to watch the impending fight.

In the centre of this rough ring of raw youth, Mick stands, looking menacing and waiting. The partisan crowd splits to allow Billy, Sean at his heel, to walk calmly and confidently through this constantly moving circle of the bustling, excited and eager mob.

They face each other down.

"Punk," calls Billy.

"Fuck off!" Mick throws back, gesturing with two fingers.

"You fuck off!" Billy retorts, two fingers of each hand stabbing the air.

Hearing and seeing Mick's threats thrown in his master's direction, the hair on Sean's back stands up. He snarls and gives a low growl; his bell ringing a warning. Billy points to the churchyard. The crowd parts. Grudging but obedient, his bell ringing an unhappy tune, Sean trots across the arena with the nobility of a prize-fighter. Ambling through the churchyard pillars, he sits on a tabletop gravestone, a perch he always takes when Billy is playing football.

Word of the fight has spread. Two crows have arrived, and like landlords, dislodge the pigeons from their perches on the chimney tops. Unperturbed by their eviction, the pigeons swoop in a circle above the tarmac stage and settle on the Thorn Inn's red ridge tiles.

Scrine steps forward, and immediately dogs start barking. Opening his mouth to make a declaration, he exposes a single black tooth, looking lonely between his purple lips. Scanning the crowd with his one good rodent eye, the other following soon after, he states that there will be "no weaponth uthed, fiths only." With every jerk of an alopecia-ravaged head, his treacherous windblown hair reveals motley bald patches. He raises his clenched bony fingers and repeats, "Fiths only, fiths only."

The right-handed Mick has arrived ready for a battle. The steel toecaps of his tatty leather boots are stained with blood. Rips in the knees of his baggy blue jeans reveal scabby black-and-blue kneecaps.

Pausing, he removes his ice-blue denim jacket to reveal a tight-fitting faded black T-shirt speckled with tiny holes, adding to the pattern created by a combination of splattered egg, soup, snot, and blood. Under his black hair, unkempt and straight, barely visible under a tidemark below each ear, is the tattoo of a bluebird. Bluebirds also fly in the crook between the forefinger and thumb of each hand. Both of his two muscular arms bear tattoos. 'Death before Employment' is inscribed on his left bicep.

More striking, however, and rumoured to have been scratched in using the serrated metal cap from a sterilised milk bottle and red ink, is the tattoo in the centre of his forehead. The ring of scarlet either, repels, allures, or mesmerises as though a mystic symbol.

With both ears embossed, along with black, wild, penetrating eyes and many facial scars on his dark gipsy complexion, Mick is a fearsome-looking opponent.

Impressed with Mick's formidable aspect, Redwing whispers to Harpy, "Geronimo."

At five foot five inches, Mick is shorter than Billy, who is five foot seven. They are both probably the same weight, but Billy is the leaner.

Locked up either in the remand or borstal system through most of his school and early adult life, Mick has never had a job. In contrast, Billy has gained an apprenticeship to drive steam engines with the British Railways. The long hours spent stoking boilers have given him a strong body and hands that are hard and calloused.

Only ten minutes earlier, fed up with sitting in his house revising for his engine driver examinations, Billy decided to take Sean for a walk when he happened across this situation. In a pale green, short sleeved nylon shirt that crackles when he moves, black Levi's, and green suede shoes with light crepe soles that give a good grip, his mode of dress is ideal for the fancy footwork he's been taught at the boxing gym. There, they use their hands to fight, not their feet. This, however, is probably going to be a different style of combat, a battle for which he's seriously underdressed.

Similar to Mick, Billy has L.O.V.E. and H.A.T.E. tattooed on his knuckles and ex-girlfriends' names under arrowed love hearts on his upper arms. Mum, Dad, and various attempts at crucifixes, anchors and unfinished names scratched in an amateurish fashion complete the artwork on his forearms. He has, on his right arm, just above the elbow, the Latin words, 'Cave Canem,' tattooed. His chest puffs up when anyone asks him for the translation, 'Beware of the Dog'. Well-trained, Sean will curl his lip and growl should any stranger attempt the pronunciation of the foreign words. Billy's blond hair is cropped short on his tanned head. When he repeatedly calls Mick "Punk, Punk," his tinny, squeaky voice sounds surreal coming from this rough, tough avenger.

An ever-growing crowd confirms that this is going to be a classic scrap and not one to be missed. Calls from parents to come home or to stay away are ignored.

In this urban theatre, the two protagonists size one another up. When he was younger, Billy attended amateur boxing classes and once fought in the Junior ABA championships. His fists, therefore, are raised in the traditional 'Marquis of Queensbury' style. His tactics are to provoke Mick into making false moves so that he can use his boxing skills to outmanoeuvre him and counterpunch.

Standing opposite Billy is a brawler. His stance compact and determined, Mick holds his fists level with his shoulders, elbows high, like he's carrying a towel draped over each forearm. Billy smiles, maybe at Mick's stance, but Mick wears a mask of determination. Not once does he take his eyes off his opponent.

They close, enough for Mick to throw the first punch, a swinging left hook that misses. Billy counters with a stiff left jab, which homes in on Mick's nose, bursting the veins in his nostrils. A tremendous cheer rings out; first blood to the Rishtons.

Mick stands back to wipe the back of his hand across his top lip. Billy honours the pause, and the Talbot takes his eyes off the Rishton for a moment to look at the blood smeared across the bluebird in the crook of his hand. The sight of his own blood provokes him into an all-out assault, which pushes Billy back against the inn gates. His wild left/right combinations land solid blows to both head and body. Caught in this gale of punches, Billy covers up, then hits Mick with a right to the body and a solid left hook to the jaw, followed by a right to the jaw. Mick's head snaps from side to side. Billy blocks a right, but Mick swings a short right uppercut that knocks Billy off his feet. Billy gets up immediately; he is hurt, but his head is clear. Using some nifty footwork, he backs up and takes in a couple of deep breaths.

"Come on Billy!" shout Ricky, Velvet, Harpy and Redwing.

On the tarmac arena between the Thorn Inn and St. James' statuesque churchyard pillars, they both square up again in the centre of the attentive crowd. Having more room to move, Billy uses his feet to good effect, making Mick miss with his haymaker right crosses.

Billy starts to box beautifully, landing solid left/right combinations to stall the Talbot's relentless advance, causing swelling and bruising around both his opponents' eyes. Blows are exchanged evenly for the next ten minutes as the fight moves back and forth between the inn gates and the churchyard pillars.

The contest ebbing and flowing, the crowd wince and cheer, following the gladiators' every move. Desperate not to miss a moment of the action, they constantly change position in the chaos of the combatants' unrehearsed movements.

In front of the inn, both fighters throw a jab but miss and come together in a clinch. Amazingly the static built up in Billy's nylon shirt sparks them apart. Mick stands there, his body hair on end. The sudden discharge causes Billy to fall back into the crowd, landing at the feet of Scream who, taking advantage of Billy's vulnerable position on the floor, kicks him in the back.

Watching in the crowd, still kitted out in his baggy blue shorts, white vest and pumps, is Ticker Barnes, leader of the Howard & Bullough gymnast team. He grabs Scream under his arm and pulls him back from the front row. And, after giving him a lecture about the unwritten code of honour associated with two men fighting—that they should be left to battle unhindered, one to one—he looks deep into Scream's milky eyes, searching for some sign of remorse, some glimmer of humanity. He receives however, a blank, careless expression that makes him feel like he is wasting his words, Ticker shoves the pitiful Scream behind him. Each gymnast, in turn, administers a clip to the back of his head as a reminder of his wrongdoing and pushes him further and further to the rear of the crowd and out of sight.

With their hands numb and gory, equally sporting bruises, welts, split lips and bloody noses, the two bare-fisted protagonists come to a halt in the shade beneath the outspread branches of the two sycamore trees that stand protectively above the stone pillars.

The earnest spectators gather around the tiring fighters. The birds crowd the higher branches of the sycamores; the cats accommodate the middle branches and two or three kids have lodged themselves on the lower limbs. Carrying this unnatural burden, the branches bend perilously low. Battling each other to gain a better view of the action, using the rubber soles of their black canvas pumps like limpets, some kids have perched precariously on the apex of the wall.

Discharges from generations of birds perching on the stone pillars have stained the flat tops white. On one of these, having claimed a prime view, Velvet is squatting on the cushion of lime. Sat on his heels, Redwing is atop the other. Both look down to see Billy jab, back up and then circle Mick. Billy lands another good jab, then blocks a left and a right hook, landing a right hook of his own. Mick backs up, throws a weak jab, and makes an uppercut. They clinch. The hatred each other holds means neither wants to feel the other's skin and like opposite magnets, they repel.

Billy jabs twice. Mick's hands start to come down. "Keep your hands up, keep your hands up," Scream yells. Mick's weak jab misses a right cross. Billy jabs and backs away from Mick's uppercut. Mick jabs and Billy jabs. Billy brings his left hand back for a quick left hook, but Mick dodges it. Back on his heels, Mick waves his left and right in pathetic punches that never get close to his wily opponent. Billy blocks a left hook and then misses with his own left before throwing another that lands. Mick again jabs weakly. Billy and the crowd sense that Mick has little fight left in him. Billy jabs Mick to the body and lands a good jab to his face. Mick misses with another weak right. Billy feints with his left, knocks Mick's left away and lands with a vicious overhand right.

As if in slow motion, Mick bends at the waist, starts to come up, but then falls sideways over his right leg, hitting the tarmac face down. To keep face, Mick rises quickly, only for his jaw to meet a short-left hook that knocks him over and on to his back. The sun sparkles through the rustling leaves like a thousand flash bulbs. Ignoring the leaves' ceaseless song, the mob scrambled to look over each other, desperate to get a mental photo of a fallen Talbot.

Supporting his weight on his left elbow, his senses dull, sweating heavily and holding his head low, Mick stares at the ground. The salty liquid seeping from his bedraggled, wet hair dilutes the drying blood that runs over his brow and dribbles down his battered face in rivulets of crimson. The bloody brine stings his swollen eyes, busted lips and the cuts on his face. Blinking, his right eye closing fast, and breathing heavily, the game is up for Mick.

Encouraged by the sight of a fallen Talbot and with stamina earned from long hours of hard work, Billy is still up on his toes but stands back, waiting for Mick to concede or get up and fight on.

Slithering from the vibrant pack, Scrine comes forward to help his flagging master to his feet and makes a determined effort to grasp Mick's right hand. He then backs away into the crowd, grinning.

His hands concealed under his elbows; Mick draws a wide sneer. His courage is miraculously restored; he raises his right hand to let everyone see the glinting brass knuckleduster with which Scrine has armed him.

Gasps of horror exhale from the crowd. They boo and shout, "No weapons, no weapons," reminding Mick of the rule set by Scrine at the start. The pigeons coo, the rooks caw, the magpies cackle and the cats hiss in disapproval.

When Scrine entered the circle, Ricky realised that he must have parked his pushbike somewhere. So, while he's helping his boss, Ricky seizes his chance to recover his stolen bike.

He tells Shirley, "I have a little job to do; I won't be long," and he leaves her side to go off on his mission.

Many of the local adults are attending the fair at the back of the church and the gymnasts have left to perform, so there's no honourable Ticker Barnes to preserve the noble art. Thus, Mick's bootlickers encourage their man with a chorus of, "Get 'im, Mick! Get 'im, Mick!"

Feeling fear for the first time in his life, Billy raises his left arm in defence against the brass knuckleduster, but the weight and force of the scything weapon break his arm above the wrist.

Holding his ineffectual arm close to his chest, his defences limited, Billy tries to keep Mick at bay with an unnatural right jab, which exposes his left side. Overcome with blood lust, his primitive instincts to the fore, Mick strikes Billy high on his left cheek, the hot metal ripping flesh from his face. Loud groans and protests erupt from the sickened spectators.

Sitting patiently on the gravestone throughout the melee, only his hazel eyes moving in the sockets of his majestic head, Sean watched and admired Billy's progress until he saw the brass knuckleduster shining across Mick's right fist. Unfamiliar with the weapon but sensing danger in the glint of the flashing brass, he became apprehensive and cringed when the first blow made contact. The scent of Billy's blood from the second strike interrupted his calm. The hair down the ridge of his back stiffened, and his top lip curled up to expose two neat rows of pure white teeth and sabre fangs. He growled, causing his ribcage to vibrate deep within his mighty frame.

Fearing the consequences should Sean attack, Billy turns his blood-splattered head to look straight into the dog's mournful eyes and gives him a firm stare to both reassure and command him to stay. Weighted by the dilemma of protection for and obedience to his master, Sean whinnied and for the first time since he sat on the cool stone, he fidgeted in frustration.

Down on one knee, trying to hold the flap of loose skin to his cheek with his good hand, a now defenceless Billy is ready to concede defeat.

In contrast, the would-be victor holds Billy by the hair, the brass raised to strike again. Sensing outright triumph, with a slow sweep of his head and through wild, glazed black eyes, the cold-blooded Mick scans the astonished crowd.

Swallowing the blood trapped in his throat, his breaking voice croaks, "I'm gonna mek mi mark o' this Rishton."

Mick's inflamed blare arouses Sean and seeing once more the brass hovering over his master's head and cowering in anticipation of another damaging blow, his Praetorian instinct overcomes his obeisance. From atop the stone slab, he produces a single bark that resonates throughout Church Kirk and beyond. The cats scarper and the birds take flight. Sean's bark was still drumming in their ears, and with his tiny bell ringing a clarion call, the crowd turned to see his one-hundred-and-twenty-pound bulk leap off the stone pinnacle. They part just in time as, on his second bound, he launches into the air, his eyes fixed and his jaws open wide.

Sean's bark also stalls Mick's vicious intent. Unnerved by the sudden silence, since the entire assembly has hushed in anticipation, Mick turns to behold the airborne hound, his ears laid back and his hair bristling. Eyes wide open, Mick is held motionless at the sight of Sean's open jaws, his red tongue flagging, breath visible, wild eyes glazed in anger, his dripping white fangs swiftly closing in.

"That's enough!" says the Reverend Samman as he snatches Mick's brass-laden hand from the jaws of the flying hound.

At the height of his leap, Sean's teeth snap shut like the jaws of a steel trap, but clenching only air, the frustrated hound turns his head to look back, incredulous as to how he had missed.

With a firm grip on Mick's wrist, the robust Reverend wrestles the blooded brass from his fingers. "It's all over," he announces with authority.

Unbeknown to the mass of noisy spectators inside St. James' churchyard, the Church & Oswaldtwistle Brass Band has struck the first chord of the hymn 'Jerusalem' and a procession of church followers has begun their march through the village in celebration of All Saints Day.

At the head, clutching the church cross, the Reverend Samman leads the joyful procession out of the churchyard. Moving forward, with the sun in his eyes, he fails to see Scream carelessly jerk his shabby coat off the pavement, but he and the whole crowd stop when a glint of light strikes their eyes and stare open-mouthed when Scream lunges forward, grasping for his lost property.

Shielding his eyes, again the Reverend misses Scream, scrambling across the grey stone flags on all fours. Magpies with their long tails dive-bomb the glinting light. From the treetops, lacquered and lustrous crows, rooks and ravens land on the inn's rooftops, croaking and cackling alarm calls. Cats dart in to scatter the birds. Barking dogs chase away the cats.

Then a black cloud drifts across the silent sky and masks the high sun. The light goes dim.

Then the silence is broken by music—a metallic clinking on the stone flags. The tune comes to a halt at the brass-buckled feet of the cleric.

He looks down and all-around young faces look on.

On his knees, wearing a culpable expression, Scream unconsciously puts his hands together and looks up at the Holy Man, pleading for mercy. Ignoring Scream, the Reverend stoops to pick up the miraculously undamaged Silver Chalice.

Cheers reverberate off the church walls, and the whole congregation erupts in celebration.

"Praise the Lord," the Reverend hails.

When all is quiet, he looks down into Scream's fearful eyes and says, "God has uncovered your guilt." Heavy with despair, Scream's head falls.

"Even in the most unlikely of souls, there lies a spark of hope," thinks the Reverend.

Holding the chalice at arm's length, the church cross in his other hand and his ornate vestments flowing behind him, the Reverend marches down the lane, leading the procession with a buoyant step. The band plays and the entire congregation and all the kids joyously sing, "And is Jerusalem builded here, among these dark satanic mills."

With the adrenalin generated during the fight subsiding, Billy's wounds begin to hurt. He feels weak and starts to shake. Drying blood has stained his green shirt brown and is sticking to his body when he sits astride the black leather seat of Jeff's Excelsior motorcycle. Holding on to the frame with his good hand to maintain his balance, his left hand is hanging at an unnatural angle, forcing him to use his wrist to support the flap of loose skin on his cheek.

Moving off, the exhaust from the green machine booms in time to the church bells as they speed towards Accrington Victoria Hospital. Acrid black gases vomiting from the tail pipe swirl in the wind, drawing a curtain across the scene. Loping along, Sean takes guard at the rear, intelligently on the lee of the carbon screen.

As soon as he is released by the Reverend, Mick absconds down Donkey Back with his two corner men.

"Gi mi 'chalus," Mick demands.

"Can't," says Scrine.

"Wha!" says Mick. "Were ta fuck, is it?"

"Re – ver – en – d's – got – it," stutters Scrine.

Fearing for his friend's safety, Screams eyebrows furrow.

"Ya nub nut!" says Mick and whacks Scrine across the face with his palm, so hard he knocks him backwards and he falls into the canal.

The two remaining troublemakers, still on dry land, hear '*Di-di-di–daa, di-di-di–daa*' trumpeting behind them. They look up the back to see Ricky speeding towards them on his reclaimed bike.

Knuckles as white as his rubber grips, out of the saddle and in top gear, Ricky speeds towards the one who had stolen his pride and joy. Startled at the speed of Ricky's approach, Scrine has to step back to avoid the skidding bike and the blinding spray of gravel. He slips and in losing his balance, he grabs hold of Mick's jacket and pulls him down, both falling into the oily canal.

Trumpeting the Morse code for victory once more, Ricky races up the dirt track with a broad smile, leaving behind him the three bedraggled Talbots scrambling out of the canal, coated in polystyrene beads stuck to the film of oil.

As soon as the procession has passed, the football game resumes, the marbles and hopscotch continue, and the street shops re-open for business. The cats fall asleep and the birds return to their endless search for food. Normality returns; Church Kirk once again is a small, quiet parish.

With another goal scored, the wall now reads: 'Rishtons 30–Talbots 29'.

"Incoming!" shouts Redwing.

Leaning forward, his head low, arms held behind him, hands wrapped around a taut rope, with slow, stuttering steps, along St. James Road, creaking under the weight of the ten-foot-long tree, Max is pulling the lead trolley.

Branches bared, the back end of their toil is supported by a hoodless pram being pushed from behind to the accompaniment of Harpy playing, 'Hey Ho! Hey Ho! It's home from work; we go.'

Axes and cleavers jammed into the trunks, jackets and jumpers slung over their prizes, the dwarf lumberjacks, with blistered palms and splintered fingers, have heaved the convoy of seven trees from the bottom of the Dunk, past Hendy's Farm and over the bridge. Leaving behind them a trail of bark and wood litter, but the smiles on their dirty, sweat-stained, flushed faces show complete satisfaction at a job well done. Max, tired from a long day's work, forces his head up and calls, "Hey! How about a push?"

Abandoning the game, the boys all rush forward to help pull, push and steer the rickety carriages past the church yard, down Donkey Back and onto the site where they will erect a pyramid of the tree trunks to form the base for a November 5th bonfire to remember. Volunteers agree to take turns standing vigil overnight to protect their hard work from raiders. And, having forgotten about Seddy who's still paralysed in his tree, people start to drift away.

Now that the game is over, Ricky goes home and straight into the kitchen to soak his hands in some Epsom salts to remove the soreness before he can begin to practice on his upright piano in the front room.

Chapter 13

November 1957 Part 7

The Evening

Today is Shirley's birthday and a party is planned to take place in the front room of the Thorn Inn. Ricky is due to play Elvis' 'Love Me Tender,' 'Young Love,' by Tab Hunter and 'A Teenagers Romance,' by Ricky Nelson. To please the older guests, he will play a couple of film scores, including the title music from the new film 'Sayonara,' with Marlon Brando in the lead role and his mother's favourite, 'The Harry Lime theme' from The Third Man.

"Tea's ready; come and get it," Ricky hears his mother shout from the kitchen.

Ricky places the piano lid down and walks into the living room. His brothers and sisters are already seated at the table and tucking into the roast chicken that, until earlier this afternoon, had been pecking around the allotment. His plate is packed with a chicken leg (legs for the boys, breast for the girls), mashed potato and home-grown carrots and peas.

To get them to eat their vegetables, his elder sister Edith bribes them with the promise of jam roly-poly for those who clear their plates. After such a long day, Ricky doesn't need any incentive. He dives into the task of clearing his plate and looks forward to the roly-poly pudding with its inch-thick suet pastry and plastered with strawberry jam, rolled and mummified with torn off pieces of a muslin sheet to hold it together while it boils in a big aluminium pan.

After the meal, Edith clears the table and Ralph lies on the couch, reading his 'Hotspur.' Sitting in his armchair, his head bent forward and shoulders warmed by a towel tucked into his shirt collar, Edgar studies the horses while Jean carefully shaves the back of her father's lathered neck.

His stomach weighted with a cannonball of roly-poly pudding, Ricky eases himself up and slowly makes his way to the front room.

The Epsom salts having done their job, he plays Mendelssohn's 'Romanze,' his fingers moving over the keys with ease.

While in the Thorn, Billy is determined to put the bad day behind him and despite the plaster cast on his forearm, stitches in his cheek and a swollen and bruised face, he is not going to miss his friend's eighteenth birthday celebration in the Thorn Inn.

On a man's 18th birthday, tradition has it that his father buys him his first drink. Knowing Little Joe is already a regular in all the pubs in Church Kirk, his dad declined the invitation, saying, "He's in the pubs more than I am."

Billy finds a seat in the corner of the taproom. With his back against the wood panelling, he begins a game of dominoes with Welly, who hasn't been home since the doors opened at eleven o'clock. With his left arm tight to his chest, lacerated fingers of his right hand almost too numb to hold the domino, Billy places a double six against Welly's six to chip out and win the game.

"Again?" asks Billy.

"Uh! Oh, all right," Welly slurs, a sure sign of a long drinking session. He pulls a Capstan from its packet and holds it between his lips while he helps one-armed Billy shuffle the dominoes, ready for another game.

"Hey up, Red," Billy greets his fellow railway worker. Billy and Little Joe are apprentices, but Red has moved upwards and holds the position of stoker second-class at the Accrington engine sheds.

"All right for a four up?" Red asks.

"Aye' Billy says. Placing their pint barrel glasses on Thwaites' beer mats, Red and Little Joe sit on opposite corners of the table.

"What the fuck happened to..."

"Mick Talbot," Billy interrupted.

"Oh! That pillock," says Red. No other explanation is necessary.

Flame-haired Red and the others shuffle the dominoes; light instantly flashes off the coal-dust tattooed into their knuckles. The stroboscopic light derails the inebriated Welly's balance and he slides sideways off his stool.
Red tries to catch him, but he's gone. Little Joe and Billy stand up and, leaning over the table, they look down.

"What happened, Welly?" asks Billy. Welly grins from ear to ear; he's held his pint steady and true. His capstan stuck to his bottom lip, he takes a strong pull on the cigarette and, equilibrium regained with some assistance from Red, he sits back on his stool. "Your fucking knuckles dazzled me," he says, rolling his eyes. The rail men look at their blackened knuckles and laugh. Little Joe only half laughed; he is more interested in the landlord's daughter, Jean. "What a good birthday present she would be," he says.

Meanwhile, in the parlour, Ricky, Harpy, Velvet and Redwing are playing 'Happy Birthday' to Shirley. All their friends and relatives remain quiet, silently revelling in Shirley's embarrassment as Ricky's broad tones sing the words with great sincerity. Sat on the floor, tom-tom drums between his legs, Redwing punches out the rhythm while the unmusical Velvet strikes a triangle.

Cackling like a Tommy Gun at one of his own jokes, Welly is past caring now and would probably laugh at a funeral. His edge worn flat cap is tipped back over his crown, and he takes a long suck on his Capstan before swilling down the nicotine with an equally long slug of best bitter.

To Billy, it seems that the bust on Bill's daughter is growing with every pint he drinks. The taproom is loud with the slap of cards, the thud of darts, and the crash of dominoes. All are contesting keenly, some laughing when they win, others moaning when they lose. Time and drinks are absorbed apace and there is a joyfully happy atmosphere throughout the building. This is Saturday night; no work until Monday. Even Sunday mornings' lie-in and time before Bill calls "last orders" are a long way off. Tonight, life is grand for everyone here assembled.

In the parlour, standing beside the piano in his Sunday best, a dark blue three-piece pinstripe suit and midnight blue trilby cocked back on his head, Jack McClintock rolls and sways. His ale-stung face is glowing. Big Jack is singing his version of 'The Lunatic Asylum. His gold medallion, swinging in time, is rubbing a crest across the front of his maroon waistcoat. With his Irish gums sucking on his loose plastic teeth, his voice sounds like a key turning a lock.

But he's interrupted.

When Harry Rhubarb bursts through the inn's front door, trips over the welcome mat, and falls amongst his harvest of fruit. Ricky stops playing and Jack stops singing.

Everyone stands up and looks down on the crumpled fruit seller. Harry braces himself on his left elbow, raises a stick of Rhubarb and points towards the church.

"Fire! Fire!" his hoarse voice cries.

Quickly, Velvet pulls the curtains apart and everyone turns to look through the stained-glass windows. All stare at the glow pouring out of St. James' tower and illuminating the churchyard.

Still on all fours, Harry hurries to gather his fruit, but the erstwhile merry-makers are desperate to get outside and witness the inferno. Rushing forward, they crush his fruit into the carpet.

Bill rings for the fire brigade and Ricky runs into the taproom to tell his dad and his granddad.

The inn is emptying fast. Outside, an assembly of regulars and visitors have gathered, some still holding their drinks. A few of the elder regulars who have worshiped at the church for many years have tears in their eyes. Everyone is staring up at the tower. It is erupting like a fiery steel furnace.

The roar, the snaps, the crackle and the popping of burning timber echo in this dreadful night.

Edgar looks at his dad, who is standing beside him and, seeing the pain in his eyes, is sure he can see for the first time a tear rolling down his cheek.

"Someone must have done something really bad today," Gilbert says.

Harpy thought of Velvet.

Bill came out of the inn and said, "My phone, it's dead! I can't ring the fire brigade," he shouts above the din.

Harpy holds his hand out, begging everyone, "Give me two pennies, and I'll run down to the phone box." Two coins thump in his palm. Holding them tightly, he sets off down the lane to the phone box. "Hey Ricky," Seddy calls from his vantage point high up in his tree.

Ricky looks up and says, "O, shit; I've forgotten about him."

"I saw Mick and Les Talbot sneak around the tower a few minutes ago," says Seddy.

"All right, pal," says Ricky, and as an afterthought, he calls to Seddy,

"Hey! I'll come and help you down after."

"Right, thanks, pal," says Seddy, his voice weak.

Ricky calls Harpy and Velvet over and together they run around the back in search of the two Talbots. But it is too dark; they can't see a thing and soon give up.

"If they are in there, there's only one man to find them; that's Redwing," says Velvet.

Ricky went to help Seddy down.

With urgency in his voice, Seddy says, "I'm alright yet, but look, up on the tower, there's a cat."

"Fucking hell! How did that get up there?" says Ricky. "Bugger knows,' says Velvet, better phone for the fire brigade."

"Harpy's already run down to the phone box," says Ricky.

Harpy flings open the red kiosk door. Immediately, he sees there is no handset. "Fuck!" he exclaims. "I know, I'll run down to the cop shop."

Staring up at the tower, Ricky turns to Velvet. "I'll bet two quid I can climb up there and bring her down." he says,

They look at each other, neither needing to speak. Velvet nods to Ricky.

Ricky runs home to change into some protective clothes. He knows exactly what he needs: an old pair of jeans with plenty of room in the legs, black canvas pumps, a jacket with a big inside pocket to put the cat in, and something to cover his head.

Approaching the police station, the first thing Harpy notices is that the blue light above the front is out. He tries the front door; it is locked. "Handy must be out somewhere. Where now?" He sets off running.

Helpless and hapless as to the cause of the fire, some regulars drift back into the bar. Word spreads that the Talbots are responsible, but the paralytic Welly does not care. He is standing at the bar, swaying from side to side next to his drinking partner, Billy, when suddenly his eyeballs turn north. He stiffens his arms rigidly by his sides, as though he had been chopped at his ankles. Unbending, he falls backwards, hitting the ale-soaked sawdust with a thud. Luckily, the collar of his donkey jacket cushions his head against the impact of the flagstone. Billy turns his glazed eyes to ask his friend what that noise was. But after a long moment of concentrated thought, "Where's he gone?" he thinks and then looks down. "Who hit him?" he says, clenching his fist, ready to fight. "Alcohol," says Red.

Unable to bend him, Red and Billy lift up the rigid Welly and wedge him into the corner of the bar. "Take him outside for some fresh air," says Jean, the landlord's daughter.

"I'd rather take you outside." Billy flirted.

"I might do it later," she teases.

After visiting the outside toilet, Scrine came in through the back door and on his way to the bar, he brushed Welly's elbow and knocked him over. Standing behind Red, who is standing behind Little Joe, Billy launches his bandaged fist past Red's ear, over Little Joe's head and into the mouth of a startled Scrine, just as he is about to blurt out some obscenities at Welly. Scrine's lips burst open, his only tooth disappears in the sawdust, and he slaps hard against the wall before sliding down slowly, settling in an unconscious heap.

"Fucking hell, you've just hit a Talbot," says Little Joe.

"Good," says Billy, "I'm just in the mood to hit a couple more. He was one I missed this afternoon." Pleased with himself, Billy made his way to the piano and picking up the microphone, he started to sing his favourite Presley song. 'When I was a lad, old Shep was a pup." His voice slurring and flat, his words gibberish, he is pelted with paper plates and waste food by those few still remaining in the best room.

At home, Ricky clasps the fleur-de-lis buckle of his scout belt to hold up his baggy jeans and carefully pulls on the pumps he uses for playing football. He then picks up a pair of his mother's leather gloves for his hands. To protect his head against the sparks, he knots all four corners of his red-chequered neckerchief and soaks it under the tap.

Although a little tight under the arms, he has decided to wear his hunting jacket, thinking he can place the cat in one of the large inside pockets, leaving his hands free for when he climbs back down. After a long day on his feet, with his verruca giving him some gyp, he winces with each step he takes. With this slight limp, Ricky returns to the church.

With the tower acting as a chimney flue, the fire is consuming all in its wake. The false ceiling, two floors, and the lantern roof have crashed down to the hot stone floor.

Ricky approaches the tower and places his pump on his first foothold, a groove worn into the sandstone by soldiers where they sharpened their swords during the Wars of the Roses. A leg up from Velvet helps him slowly start the climb up the east buttress. Carefully selecting hand and foot holds, brushing and kicking away charred wood and ash, little by little Ricky edges his way up and over the four warm buttress steps to the top. Here he pauses for a rest and to evaluate his next move. He can see the cat cowering beneath the belfry window. Immediately, he recognises it as Muriel's cat, Ginny, looking at him apologetically. Ricky smiles. "You again, eh?" The only way forward is along the narrow edge of the string course. Meowing constantly, trying to protect her paws from the heat of the stone ledge, Ginny is lifting each paw in sequence. Blinking nervously, her opal eyes are luminous as the headlights of the landlord's Morris Minor show them both clinging to the wall and ledge. His precious fingers grip the ledge, and through the thin-soled pumps, he balances on the string course with his toes.

There's a deafening crash—the heavy clock mechanism falls the twenty feet down, followed by the eerie sound of the cracking bells. The fire has blitzed the recently refurbished ringing room and the eight new bell ropes are burnt; only months earlier, the bass bell, 'Old Mary', had been shod with new bearings.

As molten lead dribbles down the stone gutters, choking and coughing in the smoke-filled air, Ricky edges ever closer to the belfry window, feeling for any raised surface or cracks between the stones to gain a grip.

Below, the crowd is silent, their eyes focused on the two floodlit figures.

The atmosphere is dense and acrid sparks rain upon Ricky's head and shoulders. The roaring fire is loud in his ears as he gets closer to Ginny. Reaching, his foot slips off the ledge. "Hoo-oo" erupts from below.

Squeezing the wall for extra grip, Ricky holds on and somehow pulls his foot back. Then, when slamming it down hard on the ledge, he grimaces, the pain shooting through his heel to his teeth. "That bloody verruca," he curses.

* * * *

For comfort, Shirley and Amelia hold each other close; their lips are compressed and their eyebrows are drawn together. With moist eyes set on the tower, they watch every movement their Ricky makes. Velvet, Harpy and Redwing are, however, remarkably at ease; they know their pal has what it takes. He might not be able to smoke or 'snog', but he has a head for heights and he can climb. If anyone can save Muriel's cat, it is their pal, Ricky.

Guarding his nose and mouth from the poisonous smoke with a cupped hand, Ricky takes deep gulps of air to recover his composure. When the pain in his heel has subsided, with the fingers of his left-hand clinging to a tiny niche in the wall, he bends at the knees and, with a swift movement, grabs the welcoming Ginny by the scruff of her neck. Promptly and roughly, he stuffs her into the inside pocket of his corduroy jacket.

A hoo-oo-ray and a round of applause break out below from the multitude assembled outside the church gate.

Shirley and Amelia sigh in relief and Muriel cups her face to cover her tears.

As he stands upright to stretch his back and with his head beside the belfry window, his eye catches the glint of something metal inside.

With the cat snugly tucked in, he stretches to reach for the metal handle he can see precariously perched on a ledge in the burnt-out belfry. But, heated by the fire, the handle is too hot to touch. With one hand holding him close to the wall, he removes his neckerchief from his head, folds it into two, and then places it over the handle. He tries again to pull it free, but finds it too heavy to dislodge from what he figures must be its hiding place.

Through the crackle and spit of the fading fire, he shouts to the crowd below. "Hey! I've found a metal looking box and its heavy. I need some help to bring it down."

In the crowd, Shirley, with Ricky's sisters, his mother and Flash all holding their hands to their faces, stared up at the tower. Anxiously watching, fearing Ricky should fall, Shirley's face wears the expression of one on the verge of tears.

Not waiting for an invitation and after a couple of slips from which he quickly recovers, the world tree climbing champion, in his moccasins, with a rope over his shoulder and his shirtsleeves rolled up under his armpits cautiously but steadily Redwing climbs up the steaming buttress wall to help his friend.

Ricky has straddled the apex of the nave and has replaced his red neckerchief on his head. He watches his pal advance and Redwing is soon on the ledge beside him. Greetings exchanged briefly and, having longer arms, Redwing takes one end of the rope and ties it to the handle of the metal box. Together, they pull and ease the mysterious box free. Once liberated, they balance it on top of the nave roof and while Ricky holds it secure, Redwing binds the rope tightly around it.

"Incoming!" Ricky shouts down to the anxious crowd below.

Sitting astride the ridge high on top of the nave, the two heroes slowly feed the rope out, lowering the casket down the steep slate roof. They jerk it over the stone rain gutter before continuing to feed out the rope until the casket nears the ground far below. When it comes within his reach, Velvet shouts, 'got it," and, taking control, lays it down to rest on a soft clump of moss.

The crowd's cheers of celebration are loud in their ears; in turn, Ricky and Redwing slowly edge their way down. On arrival at the bottom, the tower still smouldering, Muriel steps forward and gives Ricky a big kiss, a hug and a thank you as she takes Ginny from his sweat-soaked jacket. Safely in the arms of Muriel, under her gentle, loving strokes, Ginny just purrs as if nothing has happened—not a purr of thanks.

The wail of the Regent Merryweather pumping appliance siren breaks the silence.

With his face up against the windscreen, a smiling Harpy presses the siren button again. The appliance pulls up outside the church boundary wall and Harpy climbs down onto the pavement.

"You're too late," shouts Velvet. "It's all fallen down."

The fire chief ignores Velvet and orders his fire crew to commence hosing water into the smouldering tower.

The handshake between Ricky and Redwing is broken when Shirley bursts from the crowd and falls into her hero's arms. Holding her tight to stop her from falling, he feels her heart beating fast. Then, startled by their sudden closeness, they spring apart. Standing, staring at each other in a cocoon of silence amid the chaos erupting all around and unseen in the spell that holds them, Ricky sees in her eyes a need, an assurance. "Now, now, now is the time." With courage boosted by the adrenalin still pumping through his veins from the rescue, he steps close, their hands clasp, their lips touch and they kiss.

Arms around each other, they were alone, but not alone. As they press each other, they're the only two not to hear the bells crashing to the bottom of the tower.

Again, they kiss, a long kiss of youth and Ricky shivers when he feels the softness of her lips. Her chilled body welcomes his warmth. Having dreamt of this moment on so many nights, Shirley rejoices inside. Resting her head on his shoulder, she is almost pained with joy and sobs breathlessly. "There it is," Ricky mused, holding his girl tight. "I've done it; I've done it." With the weight of anxiety removed, a wave of joy swept over him. Holding her for what seems an age, he is excited as to their prospects and in his arms, he knows he holds what will be the source of all his joy and a terrific sense of responsibility overcomes him.

Amelia and Claudette's arrival breaks the couples spell and by joining in, they make the hug a foursome.

Removing her ruined gloves from her son's hands, Amelia checks for hand damage. Only when she was reassured did she let him go. Together, Ricky and Shirley go looking for Velvet, both curious as to the contents of the metal box. Walking by her side, Ricky secretly looks at Shirley and studies her lips. For sure, they had tasted raspberry.

They find Velvet outside the heavy oak doors of the nave. He is kneeling beside the mysterious looking box, his face plastered with a grin.

"All right, pal," Ricky asked, "what is it?"

"Well, according to the Reverend, it's a coffer," says Velvet, struggling to untie Redwing's knots. He raises his eyebrows and smiles. "And look, it's silver." Then, after rubbing his handkerchief across the lid, he said, "I think this is some kind of crest or a coat of arms." Reverend Samman comes forward to give his thanks, and they all stare down, admiring the fine decoration. No one's eyes are wider than Ricky's. He has never seen a 'coat of arms' before. Wondering if the Rishtons have one, Ricky promises to ask his granddad when he sees him next. Ever more eager now to know what he has discovered and if it could possibly have belonged to his family, Ricky asks, "Well, what do you think is in it?"

"Let's take a look," says the Reverend. A curious crowd has also gathered around.

Harpy produces a stout, ivory handled pocketknife. "Here, use this," he says, handing the knife to the Reverend. Velvet holds the coffer firm while the Reverend works on the small gap between the box and the lid nearest the lock with the sturdy blade. The lock proves robust, and then, with quite an effort, a crack, the Reverend succeeds. Handing the blade back to Harpy, he says, "Thanks." Then he slowly lifts the ornate cover; the silver hinges creak stiffly with age, but the coffer lid opens.

By the warm light emitted from the swan necked globe, the Reverend, Ricky, Velvet, and Shirley and the stone busts of King and Queen above the nave doorway push their heads forward to look in. Their collective heads casting ghostly shadows over the treasure, they are amazed to see the beautiful embroidered white clothes and various gold and silver coins.

Caressing the clothes, which the heat of the fire has dried crisply, the Reverend looks up into the rescuers' faces.

"These... well, they're vestments," he says.

Gilbert's face shines in the creamy light and, rubbing his hands in glee, he jumps for joy. Fondling the warm coins, he declares that "with this money and the restoration of the chalice and vestments, we can pay for all the repairs. Hopefully pilgrims will come to visit this holy site once more," he murmurs to himself.

The fire is out and although steam is still rising off the bronze bells, the red Merryweather crew, having successfully prevented the fire from spreading into the nave, has returned to the station. Everyone, including the Reverend, filters back in to the Thorn Inn, where talk is wild with speculation as to the coffer's contents and how it came to be in the tower belfry and undiscovered for all those years. Back in the taproom, old Gilbert sits quietly smiling to himself, letting the rumours buzz around the inn, content in the knowledge that he knows the answers. "Aren't you gonna tell them, dad?" says Edgar.

"Nah son, not yet; they're enjoying themselves too much. I'll have a word with the Reverend later," says the old sage. "I'm just pleased our prayers have been answered."

"Richard says there's a crest or coat of arms or something on its lid; he's dying to know if us Rishtons have one. Do we?" asks Edgar.

"Well, if it is a shield with a horizontal silver stripe below battlements and two stars above, then it is," says Gilbert.

"All right, I'll ask the Reverend to check it when I see him."

* * * *

Standing at the bar waiting for his order, Handy watches across the bar as Scrine dabs his bloody nose with a filthy handkerchief. Handy has known Scrine his entire life and his closeness to his two cousins, Mick and Les and his gut feeling is that one of them is to blame for the theft in Muriel's shop.

When Scrine turns to look at his assailant singing in the parlour, Handy's suspicions grow when he sees the plaster just inside Scrine's hairline. He removes from the envelope the tuft of hair he found in Muriel's shop and compares it to that on Scrine's head. "Umm," thinks Handy, "I wonder!" But then he surely thinks he wouldn't be so stupid as to commit a crime, having just been released from Borstal. Maybe he cut his head when Billy hit him?

Landlord Bill waits for Scrine to pay for the pint he's ordered before he releases his hold on the glass. Although feeling insulted at Bill's insinuation concerning his ability to pay, he is desperate for a drink to swill out his bloody mouth. Forcing a toothless grin, Scrine cockily digs his hand into his pocket, pulls out a red ten-shilling note and hands it to Bill. Turning away with his drinks, Handy sees the red note out of the corner of his eye and remembers Muriel's statement that she had only one red ten-shilling note and some change.

Deep from within his barrel chest, "Hold that note, Bill," Handy boomed. And placing his drink on the saloon bar, he marches around to the main bar. In a cold sweat, Scrine starts to fidget. He knows he has to get away, but there's no escape; the crowd is boxing him in. That crowd parts to let Handy through, his big eyes flashing like beacons. And placing a huge right hand on Scrine's shoulder, he says, "I think you'd better come with me." Scrine did not have to confess; the fearful look and the beads of sweat trickling down his temples gave his guilt away. Being led away, Scrine passes the Reverend, who, pointing above, says, "Again, as always, he finds your guilt."

Chapter 14

November 1st, 1957. Part 8.

Redwing Goes Scouting.

While the village folk are inside the inn discussing the evening's events, Velvet is outside the inn's front door with Redwing. "I hear you need a scout," he says.

"Ya, we think the Talbots are hiding in the churchyard and it's them who set fire to the church. Me and Ricky have had a look, but we couldn't see anything in the pitch black, so can you track them down and then give us a shout? We'll bring the troops," asks Velvet.

The land behind the church extends a hundred yards down to the canal and is littered with randomly spaced grave stones, stained sooty black and scarred by time, some blotched with various colours of lichen and/or moss.

On the upper section, Mr. Cavannagh has mown a twenty-foot-wide grass strip. The bottom half has not been used as a cemetery for many years and is overgrown with shrubbery, brambles, and long grass.

Being a man on a mission, Redwing wags a finger at Buck and says, "Sit and wait."

His belly full of crisps and beer, Buck gives Redwing a glazed look, then lays down between the churchyard pillars and tucks his nose under his thigh.

Dressed for the hunt, Redwing enters the churchyard. His senses awakened; he crosses a small area of grass when movement to his right catches his eye. He turns. Has he found the Talbots already? No, it's Billy and Jean sneaking into the dark alcove near the nave doorway; he ignores them.

Standing by the east corner of the church, only the near gravestones and the streetlights of Rishton in the distance are visible.

All is still.

Yet the guard dog barks from Pontalgh beyond the stone bridge, and nearer, from St. James' bell tower, comes the owl's haunting hoot. While below the tall stained-glass angels, his moccasins making no sound, our surefooted scout sneaks down the green gravestone path.

Kneeling on a chiselled Tom Pearson, he stares into the night's dark acre, sniffs, and, in the silent air, listens for the hidden Talbot:

No sight! No scent! No sound!

Through the rugged gloom, he navigates around those long dead, where, deep within this dark domain, weary of his elusive prey, one hand on a moss and ivied cross, he bows his native head and prays to the mighty Mudjekeewis—father of the winds of heaven.

First, a wind blast rings old Mary, then the four winds come roaring through the dark, threshing the Sycamore's, sweeping carpets of leaves in waves and sending slack church slates spinning.

Wide-eyed, our windswept scout sees dense, low, blue-black clouds mask the midnight stars, shrouding the tower and filling the air with chill and dread.

The howling tempest then dies. The winds fall to a light whisper, and calm and graceful, the silent clouds begin to swirl and, in the darkness, form an ever-brightening aperture that emits a thin beam of starlight reaching the earth, revealing the Talbot's hideaway through the clear illumination of the serrated ring of scarlet in the centre of his inglorious forehead.

Immediately, Redwing recognises the glowing tattoo, and then all of a sudden, the starlight disappears, as does the tattoo. But he's a scout and has memorised the location; he knows exactly where they are.

While the triumphant clouds return to their leisurely meanderings, Redwing rests his forehead on the back of his hand to give thanks to Mudjekeewis when he feels a tap on his shoulder. Looking back, he sees the whites of Velvet's eyes. "Where did you come from?" he asks. Velvet winks and whispers, "Catch a weasel asleep, piss in its ear."

Keeping a yard behind, not making a sound, Velvet follows in the chief scout's footsteps.

Les Talbot also saw the beam of light illuminating his brother's tattoo and naively tried to brush it off his forehead. "We've been rumbled," he says.

They bolt from their lair. Redwing and Velvet give chase.

The Talbots do not run towards Donkey Back and away along the dark canal bank where they can escape into the open country, but run through the shrub and up around the church tower into the open ground at the front of the church. Being more fleet of foot and with eyes accustomed to the night, Redwing dances around the gravestones. Catching up with the pair near the boundary wall, he prepares himself to pounce.

Meanwhile, behind him, struggling in his slip-on shoes to keep up with the swift scout, Velvet trips. Just making out a gravestone looming towards him, he sticks out a hand but misjudges the distance, bangs his head on the hard gravestone and falls into an open grave—the one dug by Edgar in the afternoon.

Running through the dark, side by side with his brother, Mick glances behind him to see a dark figure closing in. "Faster, faster, it'll be Handy Pandy," he shouts.

Speeding around a tree, they trip over, falling headlong into a tangle of brambles loaded with berries.

Instead of seeing the burly figure of Handy Pandy, it was a grinning Redwing standing above them. They become agitated, realising they needed not to have run, and try to free themselves from the bramble. But caught fast in the thicket of sinewy, sharp thorns, they are going nowhere.

Any thoughts of continuing the struggle vanish when Red and Little Joe appear, their coal clad fists clenched like knuckledusters. Others arrive from the inn, and Buck and Sean come growling and snarling. Intelligence may never have been their strength, but even Mick knows the game is up.

A little later, after everyone has left, high above, hearing some movement in the dark below, Seddy calls out. "Hello! Hello! Is there somebody there? Have you come to help me down?"

"Did you hear something?" Billy Rishton asks from the moss-covered love bed/gravestone.

"No replies, Jean."

Unnerved, Billy zips up, sits up and slips a Park Drive between his lips. "It were like unwrapping a present but not getting it all out of the box," he mumbles as he rolls his thumb over the wheel of his Zippo lighter; the spark strikes and the butane-fuelled wick ignites. Lighting his cigarette, he notices the new light illuminates the gravestone and the glow highlights a rough-hewn inscription. Holding the Zippo higher, he lowers his head, and brushing away any loose moss and soil, he moves his fingers across the inscription and reads, "Mary's... holy... well." "Fucking hell!" he exclaims.

"Nasty gob!" Jean complains.

"It's Mary's Holy Well... Not just Mary anymore; the two missing words are Holy Well. Of course, he blessed it, didn't he? Paulinus blessed the well. It's here! ... In our churchyard," he shouts.

Jean just stares at him.

Meanwhile, noticing Velvet is missing, Redwing retraces his steps in search of his friend.

In the pitch black, his head buzzing and feeling huge, but his consciousness returning, a cold Velvet asks himself, "Why am I sitting in a dark grave?"

Finding his pal, "What happened to you?" asks Redwing.

"I don't know. It must have slipped or something," says Velvet, rubbing his head. Redwing helps him to his feet and slowly they walk down the church pathway.

Standing between the two dumb church yard pillars, Billy, Redwing and an unsteady Velvet watch the full moon's slow trek across the clearing sky. "I wonder how many heads and how many feet have passed between these two pillars over the years?" asks Redwing, as he caresses the surface of the smooth sandstone.

Looking down Church Lane, they see Handy escorting the handcuffed Mick and Les Talbot away. With three arrests in one day, usually a year's tally, Handy imagines three broad stripes on his tunic. Billy explains the story about Paulinus and Mary that he read in the yellow magazine.

Ricky comes out of the Thorn, with Harpy close behind. Seeing Velvet, unsteady on his feet, "What's up with you?" he asks as he joins his two friends.

"I banged my head on a gravestone," says Velvet, still rubbing his bump.

"Serves you fucking right," says Harpy, still mad at him for wasting his last two cartridges. Not expecting the acerbic quip from his pal, Velvet looks hard at Harpy.

"Hey! Come on, my dad is putting the chip pan on," says Ricky.

"How come? There are no spuds," asks Harpy.

"Come on, I'll show you," says Ricky.

The boys cross the street to Ricky's house.

Using potatoes grown on his allotment, Edgar has the chip pan bubbling. His guests' hands are full of wedges of buttered bread filled with his luxury home made chips, to be washed down with a nightcap mug of tea.

Entering Ricky's house, the boys are greeted by the smell of hot chips wafting from the steam filled kitchen. To a rousing cheer, the boys enter the living room, which is boisterous with talk about the evening's events. Everyone is happy and joyful.

After shaking hands with them all, Ricky finds time to make himself a butty from the bowl of chips and bread from the pile on the beige tiled coffee table. He knows that Shirley has gone home with her mother and Flash, so with butter dribbling down his chin, he goes into the kitchen. "Hey dad, I've got to get up early in the morning."

"Ok, lad, I'll give you a shout," says Edgar.

Through his bedroom window, Ricky takes a last look up and down the lane, and turning to his right, his eye catches two small round lights reflecting off the street lamp, high up in the churchyard. He thinks, 'Ginny?' and then remembers, Seddy!

Fumbling in the dark, he gets dressed.

Chapter 15

We are back to July 1962. Part 4

The Final Scene.

Following the great success of the concert in King Georges Hall, Ricky and Shirley, along with friends and family, have gathered in an upstairs room of the Thorn Inn. Ricky has invited some of the musicians from the orchestra, together with their instruments, to set up a quartet on a small platform at one end of the room. With some difficulty, because Welly's wellies kept slipping on the stairs carpet (well, that was his excuse), he and Bill moved the piano upstairs. The landlord had also decorated the room with balloons and bunting to celebrate the evening.

His body tired and shoulders aching under the weight of his gabardine tuxedo, Ricky removes the heavy jacket, rolls up his sleeves and removes his bowtie.

Standing on the piano stool, he raises his hands, beckoning for attention. Seeing him standing up there, they all broke into rapturous applause. When they stop clapping and the room is silent, Ricky, feeling embarrassed, spreads his feet to steady himself, and after coughing to clear his throat, he begins. "Firstly, I'd like to thank you all for coming and for all the acclaim." Then, looking directly into Shirley's admiring eyes, he says, "As a finale, I would like to play a piece I've arranged especially for you. Oh, and thanks to Velvet for helping me with the words. This is "A Song for Shirley.""

Eager to play his harmonica in front of his home crowd, Harpy joins his pal and the quartet on the platform. Velvet and his triangle also get in on the act, with Redwing squatting below the piano, his tom-toms between his crossed legs. Together, they begin to play and Ricky begins to sing:

At an early age you walked to the stage,
With a crown on your head, not a word was said,
to collect your prize with sparkling eyes,
a sway of your hips. From raspberry stained lips
thanks, came tinkling, like raindrops, sprinkling.

The first I'd ever seen you were my Queen.
That maiden sight in the bright coloured light
was all I'd need for my love to succeed.
Our love these years is without tears,
It had endured, it was assured.

Till one false night in wine blurred sight
Cold was my thought, I'd not cared as I ought.
Myself alone I was to blame. Fearing you
a fading flame
loose your heart! We may part!

Blue! Blue I fell quite frantic.
Wanting our love romantic
I wrote this song to fix it prove it,
bind our love in toto spirit.
Shirley, hear the love I sing accept the love I bring
with every loving breath, refresh our love till death.
Oh, how we were merry, please say that we will marry.

After he sings the last word and plays the last note,
Ricky prepares himself for applause, but his ears meet only
silence. He raises his head from the keyboard to see everyone
in the room staring towards the doorway. Ricky turns to see
the large frame of Robert Talbot. Pushed into the room by
Claudette, Robert fiddles nervously with his watch chain, and
then, with an elbow from his earnest wife, his big brown
voice fills the room. "I, huh, I hope you will excuse us from
coming here," he said, taking Claudette's hand. "I know we

were not invited, but I want to say a few words, if I may?" Robert looked towards the Reverend, from whom he received an affirmative nod. Robert clears his throat and blows his nose with a sodden handkerchief. He continues, "I wouldn't have believed it only a few hours ago, but, ka-um, aa, I thoroughly enjoyed tonight's performance." He turned to the musicians. "Thanks; I was deeply moved by your playing." Then to Ricky "That Rachmany guy, is it?" Gaining confidence from the smiling faces, he becomes more animated and thumps the air. "Then at the end, those canons firing and those bells, Wow," Claudette looked up at him with a raised eyebrow. It is the first time ever she has heard him admit to liking anything 'arty'.

He moves forward and takes and shakes Ricky's hand. "I'd—um—I'd be very proud to have a Rishton as a son-in-law; well, this Rishton anyway," he says. Everyone except Gilbert applauds.

"But about the church," Robert adds soberly. And turning to Gilbert, who is standing between the Reverend and Archdeacon, he coughs, and once again, silence fills the room. Expecting bad news, the atmosphere in the room turns thick. The long pause is broken when Robert speaks again: "With the Archdeacon and Reverend's permission, I'd... I'd like to make a donation to the church fund." The archdeacon smiles for the first time this evening and nods his approval as the whole room applauds. The Reverend shakes Robert's hand, saying, "Thank you, thank you," repeating, "Bless you! Bless you."

Offering Gilbert a heavy cheque, Robert holds out his hand and says, "I hope from now on there will be no more bitterness between us Talbots and you Rishtons."

The End

Today: If you should walk towards the bridge
(its location unique), stand on her back,
and feel the suddenness from enclosure,
are moved by the distance, the green expanse;
look to the right, then to left, and despair.
Pontalgh crumbles, its history left to ruin.
The once proud farm house besieged by debris.
You won't find allotments rich in flowers,
their fruitful scents sweetening Church Kirk air.
You will find, (if you dig deep enough through

the garbage, those red bricks, the skeletons
of voles, fish and newts, ancient paths erased),
the cuckoo's manor is buried under
monstrous concrete towers that bear the drone
of tyres on tarmac, drowning out bird song.
Gone! Nature's naked charm, the realm for play,
the solace from industry, this idyll.
Adventure never glorious again!
Hard truths—the natural world has no rights!
Cold powers—dead their sense of the sublime!

*A History of Church Kirk, can be obtained from: A History of
the Parish of St. James, Church Kirk by The Rev. R.J.W Bevan and
Victor G. Palmer.

**The Triumph of Life P B. Shelley Canto XXIII